IT WAS ALL THE PIE'S FAULT

A SEXY ROMANTIC COMEDY

ELIZABETH SAFLEUR

This book is a work of fiction. Names, characters, places, and incidents are the product of the author's imagination or are used fictitiously. Any resemblance to actual events, locales, or persons, living or dead, is coincidental.

Copyright ©2022 by Elizabeth SaFleur. All rights reserved, including the right to reproduce, distribute, or transmit in any form or by any means. For information regarding subsidiary rights, please contact the Publisher.

Elizabeth SaFleur LLC
PO Box 6395
Charlottesville, VA 22906
Elizabeth@ElizabethSaFleur.com
www.ElizabethSaFleur.com

Edited by Trenda Lundin
Proofread by Claire Milto
Cover design by Cosmic Letterz

ISBN: 978-1-949076-43-1

1

Chloe had taken her eyes off her table for five seconds. That was it. Frickin' *seconds* to deliver her freshly baked pies to Scarlett at the bakery counter, and now some guy had dropped his sweaty Duke University sweatshirt over her chair.

Sure, technically, she didn't own said chair. But the little French bistro set at the front window with two chairs with iron backs curled into hearts was the place where Russell was going to propose to her. It's where they'd pick their two children's names and talk about building their dream house.

Now her chair was damp with... man sweat.

She sidled up to Mr. Perspiry Duke and plastered on the most sugary smile she could muster. "Um, excuse me."

His dark eyes slanted down at her as he swiped his damp curls across his forehead. "Yes?"

Palms together in prayer pose, she sucked in a long breath. "I have a huge favor to ask. My boyfriend and I are having our first date and I really could use this table. Do you mind?"

"First date?" He cocked his head as if he couldn't understand her. "So, he's not your boyfriend?"

"Not yet, but please?" She gestured to the small table and plunked her bag in the center. There, claimed. "It's the hearts. On the chairs."

His lips twisted as if he was barely indulging in this exchange. "Oh, a romantic, I see." His head nodded up and down slowly.

So, amused, huh? "How about I buy you a piece of pie? As a peace offering. I mean, if it won't ruin your..." she waved her hand over his incredibly broad chest, the wet stain forming a huge V down the center of his T-shirt, "...workout."

He huffed out a laugh. "I don't know." One of his eyebrows arched up. "Is it any good?"

She waved her hand around. "I bake them for Peppermint Sweet. So, of course."

"First time here."

How did anyone *not* know of this place? "Seriously? New to town or something?"

"Nope."

This man then lived under a rock—a big one given the size of him. "It's the best shade-grown coffee in town as well as the best pies. Please, it's on me."

"Okay, I'll bite. The table is yours." He moved to turn away—and left his sweatshirt, which, upon closer inspection, also had some wet stains around the armpits. *Ick.*

She lifted the sweatshirt between two fingers. "Yours?"

His lips quirked up. "You know, a little sweat won't kill you." He grabbed a fistful of his sweatshirt, and his eyes trailed down her body, lingering on her hips. Yep, that was a body checkout all right, and there was an insult simmering in his eyes.

But his judgment—the one that said, *sure she bakes,*

because look at her butt—would not douse her good mood. She cocked her head toward the counter. "The apple is particularly good. Please. I insist." Most men were easily occupied with sugar and she really needed this guy *occupied*—somewhere else.

By the time she walked the ten steps to the counter, Scarlett was already dishing out a piece of pie because, of course, she eavesdropped. Chloe swore Scarlett only worked here so she could get more info for the Great American Smut Novel she was writing in the evenings. The shop attracted a lot of couples.

A little smile formed on Scarlett's mouth. "I'd say, out of ten? His butt is a fifteen," she said under her breath as she handed the pie over to Chloe. The woman could not stop rating men's body parts.

"Hadn't noticed. Russell's is a twenty." Everything about her future husband was off-the-charts wonderfulness. "You'll see when he arrives for our date."

"I will because you know I'm the Men Measurement Master. In the meantime, do that magic love thing with your cherry pie on Mister Fifteen here. He's too fine-looking to be walking around on his own."

She glanced down at the pie. Dang it, Scarlett had dished out the cherry instead of the apple.

The man was handsome and probably didn't need the wish magic from her cherry love pie. Good-looking men rarely had trouble luring women to their man caves. "He's probably got a harem sitting on tufted pillows in his basement."

"Where do I apply?"

Chloe rolled her eyes and took the plate from Scarlett. "Promise me, save a piece of the cherry for me," she whispered and pointed at the tin sitting on the counter. "For Russell."

"Okay, but... are you suuure?" Scarlett's lashes flicked as she gazed over Chloe's shoulder. "Hi, there."

He was behind her, wasn't he? Without turning around, she could scent him—a little sweat but also some woodsy, sexy cologne. So typical of players.

Chloe gave her a tight little shake of her head and spun around, nearly sending the piece of pie right into Mr. Perspiry's chest. The guy also had no sense of personal space.

His arms shot up, and his abs caved in as if expecting an impact.

She jerked the white plate to the side. "Oh, sorry. But saved! Here." She thrust it at him. "Like I said, it's on me."

The table stealer really should have one of the other pie flavors, but she made a quick wish for him anyway: *May he find the love of his life today*—but not at her and Russell's table. The guy was unlikely to be single—tall, dark, and handsome men rarely were—but just in case, she'd do him a solid. Spread some of her magic pie wishes his way.

A roll of thunder nearly shook the room.

"Your date better get his glorious self here soon," Scarlett called over the hiss of the espresso machine.

The guy took the pie and grabbed a fork from the round utensil holder on the counter. "Thanks... um..." He cocked his head, clearly searching for her name.

"Chloe."

He stabbed the piece of pie with the fork so it stood like a flagpole and then held out his hand. "Nick." She shook it and tried to scoot by him, but he didn't let go of her fingers. "One second."

"Yes?"

"I have to taste it first to make sure it's an even exchange." He plucked the fork from its salute and cut into the pie.

Oh, for crikey's sake. "You really haven't been in here

before, have you?" She pointed at the pie. "Because *that* will change your life."

He wasted no time stuffing an oversized piece into his mouth. He nodded and chewed. "Mmm, good."

"Told you."

The man, with no sense of table manners at all, shoveled another piece between his teeth. His eyes rolled back, and more murmuring filled the air. He pointed at the rest of the pie and garbled, "I'll buy the rest of it."

"Oh, no." She waved her hands. "I need it."

"My, you like taking everything around here, don't you?" He set his pie plate down on the counter in front of Scarlett, who was darting her gaze back and forth between them. Didn't she have work to do? Like putting Chloe's pies away?

He half-smiled down at her. Oh, yeah, this guy's smile alone, even with a bit of red cherry stain, likely charmed women out of their panties in elevators and parking lots.

"Can I get a cappuccino…" He eyed her nametag. "Scarlett. Nice name."

Scarlett turned her namesake's color and waggled her eyebrows. "I think you should have more of the cherry."

Smacking his lips, he reached into his sweaty shorts. "I'm Nick, by the way. And I'll take the whole thing." He pulled out a wallet.

"No, you can't." Chloe grabbed the pie tin from the counter. He'd had enough.

Her pies were magic. They weren't the witchy, paranormal kind, but they made people's wishes come true. Nana had passed on her gift to Chloe right after her parents died with one instruction: she could only use it for the good of both people. This sweaty man wasn't one of *her people* today.

Today? Russell would eat some. She'd make the wish, and he'd identify her as the love of his life.

He'd already shown genuine interest in her. He was

always complimenting her, asking her opinion about school matters, and he'd asked to meet her here. So, as far as she was concerned, today was the day they'd push things in the romantic direction. Someone had to make the first move, so she was. No sweaty man guy was going to get in the way of her true love.

Nick's wide grin beamed down at her. "Man, you're—"

"Bossy?" Scarlett set her elbows on the counter and propped her head on her knuckles. "She's a teacher."

"That explains it. 'Sit here. Eat that.' You got the mom voice down. Let me guess… kindergarteners."

She set the pie down and crossed her arms over her chest. "First graders."

"Same thing."

As if. Besides hoovering up food like a coyote, the man was so naïve. Her students knew the difference between left and right, and heaven forbid she was late by one minute for snack time. "Hardly. My students can read sentences already."

"How impressive." He then stabbed his fork back into the remaining piece on his plate and shoved it into his mouth.

This perfect stranger had no business judging her kids or her teaching. "You remember what it's like in elementary school? Let me guess. You just graduated from it last week."

The guy chuckled—actually was tickled.

Scarlett straightened. "Chloe, by chance is that your date?" She pointed toward the large front window.

A loud crack of lightning lit up the darkening sky outside —and Russell, who was darting around the corner as sheets of rain fell all around him.

Her heart skipped and whooped inside her chest. Let her perfect life begin!

He was a few feet from the door when a streak of long, blond hair crashed right into him. *Whoa.* It'd been a full

It Was All The Pie's Fault

head-on collision between Russell and... *Oh, crapola. Seriously?*

A clink sounded behind her on the counter. "Who's the blond chick who barnacled herself onto your boyfriend?" Scarlett whispered.

The woman certainly had star-fished herself right to him. "Suzette Marie."

She and Russell laughed at one another under the awning. "Who?"

"French teacher. She started last week." It was about time Broadstreet Elementary had started language courses for the grade school kids but did they have to bring in a woman who looked like she stepped right off a European perfume commercial?

"She's hot." Nick had secured himself a second piece of the pie—drat it all—and stared hard at Suzette Marie.

Exactly the sentiment the woman had gotten from every single one of the male teachers at Broadstreet when she'd been introduced to the staff at Monday's teacher meeting last week. Stunned. Gobsmacked. Tongues hanging out. Okay, that last one wasn't true, but she saw more than a few guys swallow when the newbie turned her big baby blues toward them.

Scarlett's face went slack. "Suzette, huh? She could so turn me."

Not helping, Scarlett. "It's Suzette *Marie*." The woman had corrected Chloe when she'd introduced herself that first day.

Scarlett narrowed her eyes down at Chloe. "So, are we friends with this Suzette chick or not?"

Just because the woman was gorgeous and a little aloof was no reason to get all judgy about her—unlike the guy standing next to her inhaling her boyfriend's pie. "Of course, we're friends."

Scarlett *hmmed*. "Well, ask her how she can walk in those red high heels, will ya? I'd kill myself."

Russell yanked open the door and ushered in a soaked Suzette Marie. Her hair hung in watery curls—like a mermaid in a fairytale. She lifted a hand to her breastbone. "Oh, I am zo sorry."

Russell flashed his super-white teeth at her. "No, I'm sorry, please." He gestured her to step deeper inside—a gentlemanly welcoming of her into the shop because he was *perfect*.

Suzette Marie pulled a long, thin, silk strip from around her neck and stripped off her wet sweater, her swan neck stretching delicately. It made her drenched white blouse underneath—now so see-through you could count the filigrees on her lace bra even from where Chloe stood—slide up her flat tummy to reveal slightly tanned skin.

She dropped her sweater and scarf on the chair closest to the door—Chloe's first date seat—which covered the heart scrolled in the back.

Chloe was about to run over to meet Russell when Nick grabbed her forearm. "So, Russell Langston. Your… boyfriend?"

"You know him?"

"You could say that." He shoved yet another huge forkful of pie into his mouth. "Mmmm." He pointed down at his plate with his fork. "You could do better."

"Excuse me?"

"Not the pie." He lifted his chin toward Russell and Suzette Marie, who were smiling at one another as she shook water off her hands. "Him." He then strode away with his plate to another table off to the side.

"Want me to introduce you to Suzette Marie?" she shout-whispered to his back. He had the cherry pie, and she wasn't above moving things in her favor in the face of blond perfection blinking up at her future husband—like the woman was doing right now. Not to mention it'd keep Nick occupied.

He twisted to face her. "No, thanks. But good luck there."

Fine, she didn't need his well-wishes. She was the queen of good luck. And today's cherry pie was going to seal the deal, French bombshell dropping in like the U-bomb or not.

Suzette Marie's presence was merely a blip. A slight hiccup. A speed bump to Chloe's future as Russell's baby momma.

Scarlett ran a finger over her pink bottom lip as she smiled at Russell. "I get it now. Russell is *fine*."

Yes, he was.

Chloe pointed at her. "Scarlett, be sure to save me some of that cherry. I mean it."

"Are you kidding?" Scarlett dipped her chin. "With that Suzette chick walking around? I'm saving you the rest of the whole damned pie."

2

Suzette Marie's blue eyes locked in on Chloe. "Ah, 'allo, Chloe." She scooted up to the counter and placed a kiss on each of Chloe's cheeks, instantly wetting them with raindrops.

"Hi. Fancy seeing you here." *Why am I seeing you here?* Chloe was no fool. Standing next to a fully-decorated pastry like Suzette Marie only highlighted her plain (but nutritious) muffin-ness. That was the way the world worked, whether or not she liked it.

Chloe had to secure her spot—pronto.

"You said this place has the best coffee." Suzette Marie glanced around. "And I had to have an espresso."

Chloe swiped at her cheek. "I did." On Suzette Marie's first day, she got all welcome-wagon-ish toward the woman, filling her in on all the best places in Moorsville.

Horace's was the only dry cleaners to use.

Brickman Park had the best picnic spots.

Peppermint Sweet had the best shade-grown coffee—plus, they sold Chloe's pies. Supporting local businesses was what one did in a small town. She hadn't expected Suzette

It Was All The Pie's Fault

Marie's drop-in to be the day Chloe was trying to turn her meeting with Russell into a bona fide date, however.

Suzette Marie smiled and pointed to the ladies' room. "I will be right back."

Russell gave Chloe a kiss on the cheek. "Hey, Chloe girl. You like hot tea, right?"

She nodded, her insides turning all gooey that he'd paid attention to that little detail. "Yes, please. And perhaps some pie? I made cherry, your new favorite."

Chloe grasped the pie tin out of Scarlett's hold—the woman couldn't help hovering, could she?—and gestured to it.

Russell waved it off. "Maybe later."

Okay, there was time—after Suzette Marie had glided out the front door. She was not invited to the cherry love pie feasting.

In fact, she recited in her mind Nana's mantra to give the magic a little advance warning.

To all who eat
 This salt and sweet
 I bless your wish
 With my dish.
 If good and true
 It comes to you.
 Embrace the light
 And take a bite.

Chloe took in a long breath and let the words float out of her mind and into the Universe.

She then winked at Scarlett and moved to *their* table while Russell leaned against the counter.

Chloe smoothed down her simple black skirt. She should have worn the cherry print one that Russell had once complimented her on. She'd wanted to depict casualness, a don't-have-a-care-in-the-world vibe. Now? She would look like a JCPenney commercial standing next to a *Vogue* magazine spread once Suzette Marie returned—got her coffee and *left*.

But then Russell raised three fingers toward Scarlett. He'd placed an order for three?

Oh, no, no, no. That was one too many—waaay too many. What was the hand signal she could give Scarlett to make Suzette Marie's a to-go order?

Scarlett glanced her way and made finger jabs toward the bathroom when Russell glanced down at his wallet.

Chloe furiously shook her head. It would be bad to follow Suzette Marie to the bathroom, let her know she could be interrupting her date. Manipulating the situation was for middle school girls, not a genuine lady. Plus, Suzette Marie had to know the girl code explicitly stated *thou shall not lure away another's man*. Even if said man wasn't fully hers yet.

"Hey, Nick," Russell called over to him.

Nick lifted his chin at Russell. "Hey." Crumbs of pie dusted the sides of his mouth. *My God, he's having another piece!* This time, the apple. No wonder he worked out with such gusto, as evidenced by his sweaty clothes. Otherwise, he'd have to walk around with an Internet filter on him to display such a physique.

Chloe wasn't swayed by such assets. Give her a good man who cared about people.

Russell shot to the guy's table, and they vigorously shook hands. "See you at the game next week?"

"Wouldn't miss it." Nick rose and placed his second and now-empty plate on the counter. "Hear you have a date."

Nick glanced her way, and she quickly averted her eyes.

It Was All The Pie's Fault

He did *not* say that. The man's social skills needed a makeover.

She pretended to study the outside storm, the swaying trees, though she'd much rather be getting a view of Russell's butt in his jeans as he hovered in front of the counter.

In her periphery, she caught Nick staring at her then ambling over to where she sat. "Thanks for the pie, Chloe."

She twisted to look up at him. "You're welcome. New flavors every week. I mean… if you want more." Why was she suggesting he show back up? Because she could never stop helping, could she?

"So, about Russell…" He huffed a little and shook his head.

Of *course*, Russell. "My potential boyfriend?" Soon-to-be husband, actually.

His forehead wrinkled. "Be careful, okay?"

This man didn't know her at all. "Always am."

Nick then pushed the door open and headed out into the storm. Good, because now she could stare at Russell's great behind. His fantastic posture. His profile showing the smile he was giving a woman sitting at a small table on the other side of the shop. He oozed friendliness.

"Coffee's up," Scarlett called out.

Russell took the tiny espresso cup and a larger cup and saucer and turned just as Suzette Marie was rounding the corner. She held up her hands as if catching herself before crashing into him again. They laughed together. It was yet another shared frickin' moment… on Chloe's frickin' almost-first-date.

Maybe she should have told Suzette Marie about her interest in Russell. Chloe didn't know her well. She wasn't into sharing her life outside of work with this woman yet. But surely, Suzette Marie could tell he was meeting Chloe here on purpose.

Suzette Marie snaked her arm into Russell's and they walked over together to where Chloe sat. Okay, perhaps the girl code didn't translate so well to French.

Russell gestured for Suzette Marie to sit. "Please."

She took Russell's bistro chair. "I was to meet someone, but I got stood up." She ran a finger along her hairline. She'd pulled up her hair into a messy bun with two French braids intertwined—like something you'd see on a Pinterest post.

Russell sat the espresso down in front of her. "I can't imagine anyone ever standing you up."

Chloe couldn't believe she was sitting at her heart chairs, with the man who was going to father her children, and it'd turned into a threesome. Didn't you wait until at least your tenth wedding anniversary before entertaining something like that?

"I'm sorry to hear that." Chloe was so, so freaking sorry Suzette Marie wasn't on her own romantic rendezvous right now.

The woman waved her hand. "It's better to know who someone is right away." She lifted her tiny espresso cup with her tiny fingers and brought the rim to her pink lips.

Chloe could so get with her sentiment.

Russell darted back to the counter. This was her moment. "Yes, it is. Listen," she lowered her voice. "I was to meet Russell here. I was hoping to spend some time alone with him. You know what I mean?"

Suzette Marie blinked at her. Was Chloe speaking Sanskrit or something? "Ah, I get it. After coffee then." She curled her hand around her cup.

Russell got back to their table fast, nearly breaking a land speed record in the process. "Who was it?" He grabbed an extra chair and scraped it closer.

Suzette Marie batted her long lashes. "Who?"

He straddled the chair. "The idiot who missed a chance to have coffee with you."

"Oh, Bradley." Suzette Marie's thin gold bracelets clinked together as her hand waved in the air dismissively.

Broadstreet's gym teacher? Chloe was going to kill him. "Maybe he got hung up. Tried calling you." She pointed to the storm outside.

Suzette Marie shrugged delicately. "My phone isn't working right. I need a SIM something. I really must go to the *a-pel* store. So many things to do when one changes a country."

Chloe fumbled for her purse. "I might have Bradley's number. Why don't we…"

Russell's hand descended on hers and his brows furrowed though he kept his eyes on Suzette Marie. "You deserve better."

"Yes." Suzette Marie delicately sipped her espresso. "I do. I need a gentleman—someone more like you." Her lashes fluttered again.

Russell cocked his head. Ah, interest piqued—freaking great.

He leaned forward. "We're glad you're here. I can run something by you ladies. About the kid's show right after spring break."

Suzette Marie placed her hand on Russell's forearm. "I'd love to hear it."

He smiled at her and made no move to remove her touch.

Chloe was a tad rusty—okay, rusted shut—about dating matters. When would she have had time to practice between baking and teaching first graders? However, there was one thing she knew. Dates were supposed to include two people. It was supposed to be Chloe and Russell at Peppermint Sweet's little bistro table in the front window sitting on the two heart chairs—and only them. Two chairs. Two people. *Two of everything.*

But, here the three of them sat, with Suzette Marie's hand on Russell, who was clearly trying to make the new girl feel better about being stood up. Like he was the romantic Red Cross or something.

One of Russell's dark curls drooped over his forehead again. "So, what do you think?"

What *think*? Chloe hadn't been listening to his ideas. She nudged Suzette Marie's foot under the table—a reminder of the *femme* code.

Russell's brows pinched together. He leaned over a little to check under the table then glanced up and smiled at her. *Gah, wrong foot.*

"Such a brilliant idea, Russell." Suzette Marie set her cup down with a delicate clink and dabbed her mouth with a napkin.

He slowly straightened up, his eyes following every single pat. He swallowed—hard. "I think the kids will love it, too. Painting their own sets, even writing the script. We could get all the departments involved then, from shop to English—"

"And my students could contribute some refreshments, perhaps from France?" Suzette Marie's eyes widened, and her hand moved to his forearm—again.

Desserts were Chloe's department. "Actually, I'll be supplying my pies."

Suzette Marie and Russell turned her way—finally, after looking at one another far too long.

"Chloe's pies are great." Russell grinned at her, which turned her insides to melted butter. "They sell them here. She's really talented."

"Thank you." She hadn't realized he'd noticed. He seemed to be perpetually training for some athletic endeavor or her pies had been devoured in the staff lounge before he got

It Was All The Pie's Fault

there. She really needed to be better at saving him a piece. And today, she'd brought an entire pie just for him. At least, until Mr. No Manners got a hold of it.

Suzette Marie blinked. "So, no room for both my and Chloe's treats?"

Oh, a pout, too. Was there anything more lethal than the French pout—something the woman had done at least three times since commandeering Russell's spot? Not that Chloe was counting or anything.

"Always room for both." He winked at her—magically twisting Suzette Marie's pretty little scowl into a smile.

Chloe should have worn lipstick.

Suzette Marie's hand found Russell's forearm again, only this time, it stayed. *"Parfait."*

Oh, she was presenting a delicious parfait alright, a truly dense one. Chloe kept her smile on—firmly. "Speaking of pie. Russell, how about that piece now?"

Suzette Marie ran a finger along her espresso cup. "Oh, not for me. I have to watch my waistline." She glanced at Chloe's torso. Yes, that was a definite check-out-her-waistline moment. That had been twice today.

"Russell?" Chloe asked. "The cherry is fresh."

Russell patted his stomach. "Normally, I'd love to, but I ran five miles this morning. And my cheat day is Sunday this week."

"Oooh, five miles." Suzette Marie cooed, her lips forming a perfect pink "O." Did this woman have anything in her repertoire that wasn't so... so... *flirty?*

Scarlett was at a nearby table, rubbing the same spot over and over with a cloth, her eyes firmly on Suzette Marie. She rolled her eyes at Chloe.

Chloe raised her eyebrows. What did Scarlett expect? It wasn't Chloe's fault a French croissant joined her and Russell —and she'd missed his *cheat day.*

She should have made her lemon-coconut meringue pie. It warded off evil spirits—like the ones that must be circling over her head right now.

"I'm so glad Chloe mentioned this little place. So romantic." Suzette Marie's mouth twisted into a smile, which Russell returned. "Reminds me of my town in France."

"Do you miss it?" Chloe could totally scrape together plane fare—and they had daily flights to Paris, right?

"It was time to move on." Her delicate hand circled in the air again, as if she couldn't be bothered. "The men here—except for Bradley, of course—are so much more... how do you say..."

Russell had leaned forward as if hanging on her every word. Yes, that's what he was doing... *hanging*.

Suzette Marie finally settled on, "Sweet."

Russell beamed in the woman's direction. And there went her wandering hand again—this time, drifting to his shoulder. Swear to God, if she squeezed him...

How had her date gone so off the rails? Women didn't do this kind of thing to each other anymore.

"I am sure Chloe would agree with me, no?" Suzette Marie cocked her cute little chin Chole's way. "Men like Russell?"

The two of them kept sneaking glances at each other.

Chloe twirled her cup on her saucer. "I'd say the men here are gentlemanly. They know when to focus on a woman—and when not to." She raised her lashes and glared at the woman who could not get a clue. What did a girl have to do to have a first date? Brand his forehead?

It then dawned on her. She had violated one piece of advice Nana had given her long ago: "Do not advertise your man." And what had Chloe done? She'd hand-painted a billboard for the woman.

In addition to the location of Peppermint Sweet, Chloe

had told her Russell Langston was perfect. He oozed charm. Being the first to say hello to people. Asking questions. Showing such interest in others.

That, and his walk. It was this lumbering casual-cool thing—like he hadn't a care in the world. She may have even sighed the description to Suzette Marie.

Russell leaned back in his chair and appraised Suzette Marie. Chloe had studied his face long enough to know when he was ruminating. His big brown eyes got a slightly hungry look, and the words swimming in his mind right now broadcast from them entirely too strongly. He was thinking Suzette Marie was most definitely flirting with him—*luring* him to do something.

And he? *Challenge accepted*, said his eyes.

This could not be happening.

It would be so uncharitable to toss Suzette out into the storm, wouldn't it? It might make that white blouse of hers even more see-through than it already was. Yes, pushing Suzette out the door, maybe even with a big karate kick, would mean her beautiful red suede heels—*worn on a freaking Saturday*—might be ruined. Her super-tight jeans might cling more to her frail body. Her make-up would... Wait, the woman wasn't wearing any.

Defcon one.

Russell grasped Chloe's hand and squeezed. "You okay?"

There went her glare—and her overreaction, both now puddled at her feet. And any thoughts of branding vanished. The man knew what to say and when to say it. See how perfect he was?

"Well," Suzette Marie pushed her chair back and rose. "It looks like the rain has stopped. Time to go get my manicure."

Well, well, there was a God. Maybe she heard Chloe's thoughts, or the prayers every molecule in her body was chanting up to the heavens to please get this woman back out on the street already were answered.

Russell jumped to his feet to help pull out Suzette Marie's chair. "Scaring you off so soon?"

"Oh, I don't scare so easily." Suzette Marie smiled down at Chloe. "No one should."

She was right. Chloe rose from her chair, too. "See you Monday, *Suzette*." For our chat about the girl code because Chloe was most definitely filling the woman in about her feelings for Russell.

"You were right, Chloe. This is the best spot in town." Suzette Marie then glided out the door.

Only then did Russell focus his big, chocolatey eyes on her. "That was nice of you, Chloe. Telling Suzette Marie about this place."

Oh, yeah? She was sooo nice. She settled back down on her seat. "Trying to be neighborly." Though she might have to be less "visitor center" and be more "neighborhood watch" in the future.

His hand reached out and grasped hers. He curled his fingers around hers, spreading his warmth into her hand. "I'm really glad you met me here. I've wanted to talk for a while."

And just like that, her insides went to goo. Her date was back.

"Want another tea?" He pointed at her empty cup. "I have some other ideas we can mull over." He glanced around. "Maybe we could hold all our show meetings here."

Yes, yes, yes! "That would be great." Place established. Suzette Marie vanished.

Russell rose and headed to the counter. While Greta, the shop owner, attended to him, Scarlett scooted over.

She sat down across from Chloe. "Girl, you need to bring out the claws."

It Was All The Pie's Fault

Chloe shook her head. "That's a bit much. I shouldn't overreact." Chloe'd had a momentary lapse in the self-esteem department. That was all. She could reclaim it.

"That woman almost crawled into his lap. I saw it with my own two eyes."

Perhaps the woman likely had flirting in her genes. "It could be a beautiful French woman thing. It wasn't her fault Russell couldn't keep his eyes in his head."

"Oh, I'd say he was going to have trouble with both of his heads... soon." Scarlett slapped her forearm. "And *you* are beautiful."

Chloe let her gaze drift back over to where Russell stood. No, *he* was beautiful.

"Chloe. Look at me. You need to fight."

Her insides bristled, and she turned back to her friend. "I hate confrontation."

"Other than he's good-looking, what do you see in this guy anyway?"

She glanced at Russell and then scooted her chair closer to Scarlett. "Well, for one, our lives would mesh beautifully. We're both teachers, love kids, love this town. It's like we were designed for one another. Not to mention he's so giving. He's always the first to volunteer for charity events and he mows his great aunt's lawn like, every weekend. You can tell a lot about men who take care of their families."

"Family. I get it. That's what you want?" she asked gently.

"Yes." She rubbed her sternum. Three years after her Nana's death, the last family member she'd had left, and the hollow pit in her chest still ached. "Ever since Nana died, I see how life can slip away in an instant and you're left with nothing. I want a family of my own."

"And you're sure he wants that, too? I'd hate to see you waste your time—"

"He told me." He had one night. They'd both ended up in

the parking lot after a parent-teacher conference. They were the last to leave—or so she thought. He would have definitely kissed her then given the way he kept leaning toward her, but Bradley bounded out of the building suddenly and broke the spell.

Scarlett's eyes grew wide. She straightened and stared over Chloe's head. Chloe turned and found Suzette Marie standing behind her.

The woman smiled at both of them and leaned down to whisper to Chloe. "I came back because I forgot this…" She reached down and grabbed her scarf that had slipped to the ground. "Don't worry. I understand. You want Russell." She then winked and strode out the door.

Chloe turned to Scarlett. "See? She wasn't trying to steal him. I overreacted." In fact, she'd bake her a pie for Monday. A pre-thank you gift for bowing out.

Scarlett shook her head at her. "You didn't believe that, did you?"

"Of course, I did. Maybe she was just testing Russell. Seeing how he'd react. And she probably could use a friend. She's new to town." Chloe knew more than most what it was like to spend every night—and holiday—alone.

"At least talk to Suzette. She was totally not cool today."

"I will. On Monday." She'd be civil with Suzette Marie. Tell her how making pouty lip origami toward him wasn't helping Chloe's cause at all.

But for now, she was going to sit here and enjoy her alone time with Russell. Move her almost-date into definite-first-date material.

"Ladies." Russell peered down at them, a cup of tea in his hand. "Was that Suzette Marie I saw? Everything okay with her?" A deep dent formed between his brows.

"Everything's perfect." It truly was—now.

Scarlett scooted away but not before giving Chloe another skeptical eyeroll.

"Good. It was nice of you to welcome her, Chloe. You're a good person." He settled into the chair. A shock of hair fell over his forehead.

"I try." She lifted her new cup of tea to her lips.

"And you're…"

She leaned forward. "What?"

His beautiful eyes met hers again. "You are a woman that…" his gaze fell to his hands cradling his cup, "a man would be crazy to stand up. Like what Bradley did today." He scoffed.

"I would never go out with Bradley."

A half-smile formed on his face. "Good. I wouldn't want you to."

A comforting warmth grew in her belly. She hadn't been imagining his interest.

But then, Suzette Marie knocked on the glass window and waved—and Russell beamed a face-splitting smile back at her.

3

Nick spun his hand on his steering wheel and eased his car into his office parking space. "Yes, I'm getting out. In fact, I stopped at a coffee shop. Sweet something."

Daphne laughed in his ear. "Only you, big brother, would think stopping for coffee on your way to work was getting a life. But let me guess, you also had sugared scones."

"Pie. But I'll have you know, dear sister of mine, I also ran several miles this morning." Of course, he destroyed the caloric deficit with three pieces of pie, but he couldn't help himself. That girl Chloe could bake. Plus, she got a cute fire in her eyes when he balked at her orders.

With a chirp of his key fob, he secured his car and strode to the stairwell. With any luck, few people would be inside his office building. Idle chitchat wasn't on today's docket.

"So, any sign of the blue devil?" Daphne's ex-husband would be stupid as shit to be within a hundred miles of her given the protective orders against him.

"Nowhere to be found."

"Good. You still carrying my present around?" Since the guy was so fond of blacking Daphne's eyes, let's see how he liked his own nearly burned out of his skull with mace the next time he tried something. Prison was his next step if the man so much as crossed her thoughts.

"Yes, dear brother."

She was humoring him, wasn't she? "And the little man?" His nephew had at least had few encounters with the abuser. "If you move to L.A. with me, you know, Benjamin could start over."

Daphne heaved a sigh. "He likes his school."

"He'd love a school in California even more." Once he secured the L.A. office gig, he could easily bring Daphne and Benjamin out with him. "Sunshine. Skateboarding every day. And the cute girls born to Hollywood stars. I'll figure out how to introduce him to the cast of that Nickelodeon show. What's it called?"

"*Mason's World*. And he's ten. Girls aren't even on his radar."

"Uh-huh." By the time Nick was ten, he'd seduced the Spice Girls and every model in his mother's *Vogue* magazine —in his dreams, of course.

He pushed open the office door with his back, twisted, and came face to face with one of his senior partners, Hank Carter.

Shit, of all the people to run into today.

"Gotta run, Daphne." He killed the call.

Hank eyed his T-shirt and shorts. "Nick. Working out?"

"Was. Just picking up some papers I forgot."

"Good. Rain's stopped and it's turned out to be a beautiful day."

"I won't be long. Headed out?" God, let him be. Nick had work to do, like re-upping Daphne's restraining order for her for a second time. He was getting too good at making that happen.

He also had research to do to help his neighbor Claire with a potential wrongful termination claim—off the clock.

"Golf. You should consider taking it up."

In his next lifetime, perhaps, and only then if they held a gun to his head. Such a waste of time. "I'll do that."

"Glad to hear it." Hank nodded. "Don't want to end up like old Weeks."

Ah, thirty seconds into this hallway run-in, and the partner who died in the office alone, single, and jaded at age forty-nine had risen in conversation. A record for Hank, who usually waited a few more minutes before reminding Nick not to end up the same. Made for bad press, for one. Hence, the partner's new "no weekend working" rule.

Of course, the man was here himself, even though he'd made a huge deal of Nick's "lack of work-life balance" during his last review. If he wasn't visiting his sister, he was in the office. It's what someone in their thirties was supposed to be doing—establishing himself and all that crap that actually wasn't crap at all. Work is how life worked.

"Golf's a big game in the west, and it'd be tragic to waste all that California sunshine."

"Wouldn't dream of it." Rather, he dreamed of drinking in the sun from his new California partner's corner office lined with windows—once he finished his penance in this tiny town.

He'd agreed to delay his transfer to the L.A. office because Hank and company had dangled a better carrot before him: prove he could handle the workload without killing himself here and get placed in California, not as an associate but as a full partner.

Deal. Struck.

Five more months to go in this place time forgot with its cute coffee shops and town squares. Or less. He had enough vacation days saved up to lop off at least four weeks of that prison-worthy sentence.

Hank slapped him on the shoulder and then strode out the door.

Of course, he turned down the hallway to his office and ran into yet another partner, so he bagged working in the office altogether. He loaded up his briefcase. Working from his dining room table was as easy—and away from eyes that were far too interested in his personal life, like how he was still single, another thing brought up time and time again.

On the way home, he had to go down Meckleson Street and pass by Peppermint Sweet. In fact, maybe he'd swing inside and grab one of the pies that Chloe chick had made. His sweet tooth was a demanding sucker.

As soon as he turned onto Meckleson, a van pulled out of a space right in front of the bakeshop. He pulled in. It'd be a shame to let that bit of good parking fortune go to waste.

"Hi, handsome." Scarlett greeted him with a huge grin. She was a harmless flirt, unlike what he'd witnessed from that knockout who joined Chloe and her Russell. That blond girl was Olympic-level.

"Chloe's in the ladies' room."

He glanced at the baked goods under the glass counter. "Oh?"

"Russell left." She sighed dramatically. "Left our little magic pie queen all to herself. Something about catching a basketball game or something."

Just thinking of the guy chafed his testicles a little. "Just here to buy a pie."

"We only have two slices of the apple left."

He pulled out his wallet. "Seriously?"

"You gotta get your bid in early around here. Chloe is a baking celebrity."

A loud *ahem* sounded over his shoulder.

He spun to find Chloe behind him. "That's stretching it," she said. She crossed her arms over her breasts once more. Trying to hide them, perhaps—though why she'd want to cover up those glorious assets, he'd never know.

"So, you came back for more pie? Three pieces weren't enough?"

Sassy, alright. "You counted."

She stepped closer and shrugged. "Yes, it's amazing. I can count. *Like my first graders can.*"

This chick was hilarious.

Scarlett leaned over the glass countertop and stuck her face between them. "Oh, that's because she needed to make sure Russell got at least one piece of the cherry. Ya know, for the magic."

Chloe threw her a wide-eyed glare.

Magic? Someone had inhaled too many espresso fumes. "The what?"

"Never mind." Chloe waved her hand. "Sorry, you missed the pie. Maybe next time." She turned away.

"So, how'd it go with Russell?"

She glanced over her shoulder. "Fine."

Sure, it was. Nothing was fine given that blond sitting with them. The sex kitten wasn't his type but was definitely Russell's. Any woman genetically gifted on the outside was, and Russell likely had ignored Chloe most of the time. Totally not cool if their meeting truly was a date.

Chloe strode back to him. "In fact, we have our *second* date next weekend."

A little *hmm* left his throat. "Not his usual style." Then again, this girl likely counted tripping into someone as a date.

A cute frown line formed between her eyes. "What? You have a thought?" She moved closer—with conviction.

Ah, so she thought she could pump him for info on

Russell. He didn't have time to school this lost woman on men like that. "Nothing. I'll take those two pieces, Scarlett." He glanced at Chloe, who continued to stare up at him as if he was a romantic oracle or something. "That way, you can say you sold out."

"They do that every weekend." Chloe shook her head. "I mean, not to brag but—"

"I know what you meant."

"So…" A smile dawned on her face, one eerily similar to when his sister Daphne had wanted to know all about his high school best friend.

She ran her finger over the countertop. "How well do you know Russell? You go to school together or something?"

Oh, man. He did not do this crap. He shouldn't have asked her how it went with the guy. He'd rather oppose the most strident counsel from one of the big five before the Supreme Court than face the insistence a female could have when they thought one guy had the goods on another.

He handed Scarlett a twenty-dollar bill. "Thought he was your boyfriend. You should know him better."

"I know enough." She leaned an elbow on the counter, which only deepened that crease between, quite frankly, a spectacular pair of boobs. He was usually an ass man, but he couldn't help but admire her front.

Scarlett pushed a white box holding his sugar fix across the counter. "Here you go."

Chloe's fingers touched his forearm. "But if there is anything—"

He whirled on her, and her words stopped. "The only thing you need to know is you could do better. So could your blond friend." Russell Langston was the worst kind of man. A guy who pretended to be a boy scout but invited everything in a skirt into his tent.

"Oh, they're not friends." Scarlett handed him some change. "She's the enemy storming the fairytale castle."

He pocketed his change. "Then let her because, like I said, you deserve better."

Chloe snorted. "Like you?"

He shook his head. "No." He wasn't a boy scout either.

She crossed her arms once more, and fire returned to her hazel eyes.

He raised one hand in defense. He wasn't trying to hurt her feelings here. "You're probably a wonderful woman." He lifted his pie box. "You certainly have some skills."

"I have many, which makes me perfect for Russell."

He leaned down close to her ear. "You may be perfect for him, but he's not perfect for you." Then, not wanting to get into it further, he strode away with his pie box.

"Hey," Scarlett's voice rang out. "You forgot to tell us your wish. So, Chloe can—"

"*Scarlett,*" Chloe's voice hissed.

He paused at the door, turned, and pushed it open with his back. "I wish for you to meet the perfect man for you."

"See?" Chloe called out. "It's already working. *Russell.*"

"Whatever you say." Jesus, he sang the words. No man worth his salt *sang*. Women made him do stupid things.

He let the glass door shut behind him, the bell chimes fading in the street sounds.

Women and their delusions.

4

Chloe stomped on her brakes hard and nearly pitched herself through the windshield. *Whoopsies.* Her usual parking space, the third one from the entrance, was occupied—by a silver Kia with an Ace Rental sticker gracing its cute little bumper.

The car had to be Suzette Marie's. So, the woman hadn't yet secured a permanent vehicle. *Does that mean she wasn't sure she was sticking around?*

Chloe pulled into an empty spot down a few spaces from her usual one. Never mind. A parking space meant nothing. Not. A. Thing.

Who cared if she'd worked hard to establish her parking place next to Russell's black Audi? It had taken two pies for Bradley to move his honking big truck down two more spots. You'd think a gym teacher wouldn't have minded a twenty-foot-longer walk, but no. He'd required an apple pie and a chocolate cream to make the move.

Chloe lifted the pie from the passenger seat and cracked open the door.

Suzette Marie was new to town, didn't have many

friends, and her flirt-a-thon yesterday must have stemmed from a deep need to be liked right away. Chloe would befriend her for real, starting with a pumpkin pie.

Suzette Marie needed just one bite, and then Chloe's wish for her—to find her place at Moorsville and find a man other than Russell—*would* work. It wasn't cherry, but pumpkin symbolized rebirth, and it was low-calorie. Then Suzette Marie could go rebirth a new life with a new man without jeopardizing her dedication to the size of her waistline.

Mr. Markinson, the school principal, stood near the bus drop-off point, greeting the final busload of kids. He was a great principal, always saying good morning to every student who arrived.

The man had lost his wife a few years ago, and it had unleashed a latent Don Juan, according to teacher gossip. He'd even asked out some of the higher grade teachers.

Maybe Suzette Marie needed a tour guide of the local area. Mr. Markinson was quite a bit older than her, but maybe she fancied older men.

In fact, maybe she'd bake a cherry pie for him.

When Chloe got to the staff lounge, Suzette Marie's perfume instantly assaulted her. The woman's long blond hair dripped down her shoulders, and she was fiddling with the coffee machine.

"Ach." She scoffed and waved her hand at the machine. "What is this? I must bring in a real espresso machine."

"That'd be great." She set the pumpkin pie down.

Suzette Marie turned her way. "Oh, 'allo Chloe. How do you drink this?" She lifted the paper cup from the dispenser with two fingers and placed it in the small sink to the side of the offending machine.

"I'm a tea drinker, myself." Chloe shone a bright smile her way. Friendliness should always precede tough conversations. "Pie?" She lifted the pumpkin. Sugar helped, too.

Suzette Marie frowned and shook her head, which only made her impossibly more adorable. "I wish we could have some of that espresso from that cute little shop where we met Russell on Saturday."

"Um, speaking of which, thanks for exiting the situation." She twirled the ring on her finger.

Suzette Marie cocked her head like she didn't understand.

"I know we don't know each other well, but I appreciate you seeing I was on a date at Peppermint Sweet. I mean. Eventually. I mean, it kinda got awkward. I mean, flirting with him so much." She added a little titter at the end.

"I wasn't trying. I am who I am. If he was truly on a date, he should not have been interested. But... don't worry. I am not interested in Rus-*sell*." She shrugged delicately. "Even if I got this sweet note from him." She reached into her skinny jeans back pocket and pulled out a little slip of paper. "He wants to help me with the *a-pel* store."

The direct approach was going to be necessary. "Oh. Well, I'm exploring a relationship with him, and he asked me for another date." There, brave. Direct. Scarlett would be proud. "Even if it was hard to get his attention with you there." Because *come on*.

Chloe's first date with Russell had morphed into a ménage a tròis with a woman who'd gotten the naturally shiny hair, the big blue eyes, and the French pout. If one was born with a French pout, she really should toss one of the other assets back to the gene pool, or if not, let some men out of her fishing net. That was only fair. Testing him with said assets wasn't a friendly thing to do.

Suzette Marie eyed her. "You are too hard on yourself. We all have our talents. Like your baking."

Chloe knew full well she had talents, but she was a little surprised Suzette Marie noticed. "You know about that?

Speaking of which..." she gestured to her pie, "sure you don't want some?"

She shook her head and smiled. "Russell told me about your treats. He also said your students love you."

"He did?"

'Of course. So, don't worry. We are only friends, Chloe. Like you and I." She placed her hands on Chloe's shoulders. "I know you like Russell, so do you want to know what I would do?"

Chloe vigorously nodded. In fact, she wanted to go get a pen and paper. This woman clearly had man-luring skills, and learning new skills should be a lifelong practice.

"Be yourself. Smile. Flirt. Let them do something for you. Play a little hard to get."

She blinked at Suzette Marie. The 1950s had landed at Broadstreet Elementary and no one told her, had they? Back then, women pined by the phone and waited for a man to ask her out. Is that seriously what Suzette Marie thought worked?

"Is that what you're doing with Bradley? Playing hard to get?" The man hardly seemed to be falling in line.

"He's sweet. We'll see what he does, too. I have to get to class now." The woman winked one pair of the longest eyelashes Chloe had ever seen on a woman. "But remember, when men are interested, they let you know."

Chloe was on the right track then. "He asked me to meet him at a basketball game party at his brother's house this weekend."

"See?"

"Um, thanks, Suzette Marie." *I think.* She had a point about men and their desires, but her ideas seemed a tad old-fashioned.

Be herself. When was Chloe not? So, check.

Smile. Check.

Let Russell do something for her. Buying her tea counted. Check.

Play a little hard to get. Dang it.

But this whole "wait for the man" thing? Chloe tapped her lips with her finger. She could let Russell decide, alright—with a little help. It was time to bring out the big pie guns.

5

Chloe straightened her cherry-print skirt—the one Russell had always complimented her on—and pressed the doorbell again. Perhaps no one heard the chimes the first time. A bunch of guys watching a March Madness basketball game could drone out a jet engine if the plays were good enough. But Russell has asked her to meet him here, even sent a follow-up text message this morning about it, and here she was.

She stepped backward to peer into the living room window, and the tinfoil over her cherry chocolate pie crinkled. The sun's glare only revealed people's silhouettes milling about inside. *Come on. Someone answer the flipping door.* Time was a-wasting, and she had a man to secure.

She pressed her ear to the door to listen for footsteps, and it fell away under her cheek. She bolted upright and nearly lost her hold on the pie.

"Chloe?" Chad's wide smile at least seemed happy she'd come to his little man cave gathering.

"Hi! Um, yes, Chloe Hart. You remembered my name." Russell had only introduced her to his brother once, and it was in passing. "I'm to meet Russell here." She peered around his shoulder.

"Oh. Sure." He stepped backward and gestured for her to step inside. "Is that a—"

"Pie." She lifted it up but didn't hand it over. Guys inhaled treats, and this was her future boyfriend's pie. "I know how you guys always get hungry when winning."

It wasn't the main reason that she'd brought the pie, but it wasn't a lie, either.

Chad blinked a little and shrugged. "Okay. Kitchen, I guess."

The television set roared and Chad spun to the living room as if yanked back by a bungee cord. "Whoa. What'd I miss?" His face focused on the ginormous flat-screen television.

Go play testosterone games, she thought. She could find her way around. She rounded the entranceway corner and her eyes zoned in on only one man—Russell. He sprawled on the couch—and he wasn't alone.

Well, well. Look at that. Suzette Marie was here. And sandwiched between Russell and another man she didn't recognize. Whatever happened to "I'm not interested?"

That was okay. The pie had entered the building—and on his *cheat* day.

Chloe plastered on a smile. "Hi, guys."

Suzette Marie's eyes sliced Chloe's way immediately. In slow motion, a sly smile inched up on her beautiful face. She waved and then adjusted her off-the-shoulder top that sported a big flounce around the neckline. On Chloe, the baby doll top would make her breasts look like she was breastfeeding a little one at home.

She lifted her pie toward them. "Cherry," she shouted into the noise. "With a chocolate crust." *Double love magic.*

"Hey," Russell mouthed.

Hey? Is that all she got? Chloe shrugged off her coat and draped it over a nearby chair.

The dozen other guys in the room pumped fists and shouted *come-on*s and other stuff as if the basketball players on the screen could hear them. They completely ignored her, which was fine by her.

She maneuvered her way over to Russell and Suzette Marie, careful to avoid the flailing arms of the guys hovering around the large flat screen.

"Good game?" She stopped in front of Suzette Marie's outstretched leg, clad in skinny jeans.

"I don't understand any of this." She waved her delicate hand toward the screen. "Bradley was supposed to be here and show me what all this flapping is about."

Oh. She was here to meet Bradley—thank God. But the man better get himself here pronto. Her first graders told time better than that guy.

Russell leaned forward to put his elbows on his knees and peered around her toward the TV. "It's a good game. Getting better now that Duke is behind—like, way behind."

A roar came through the screen, followed by the guys in the room hooting and high-fiving one another. Russell threw himself against the back of the couch with a big *aww man*, and his hand landed on Suzette Marie's knee. It stayed there.

"Chloe?" Suzette Marie's face came into view. "You alright?"

Chloe's lashes lifted. She'd been staring at Russell's grip on Suzette Marie's leg.

She lifted the pan. "Pie, Russell?"

"'Ow sweet of you." Suzette Marie reached for the tin, and out of sheer reflex, Chloe jerked it back. That was mistake number one.

First, it looked like Chloe wasn't a sharer. She most certainly was a sharer—except for her future boyfriend.

It Was All The Pie's Fault

Something Suzette Marie obviously didn't fully grasp by her willingness to be groped by the father of Chloe's future children.

Second, she yanked back so far, one of the gesticulating guys stepped back into her. He knocked her elbow forward so hard, her pie went flying—right into Russell and Suzette Marie.

Their mouths dropped in perfectly matched "O's" and their hands raised as if trying to shield themselves from the pie's beeline for them. Its trajectory, however, could not be stopped or avoided.

"Merde." Suzette Marie shook sugary goop and crust off her hand while a red juice stain spread like wildfire across her flouncy top.

Chloe half-gasped, half-chortled, and quickly sealed her lips at seeing Russell's face. His eyes widened up at her as if accusing her of coating them in cherry juice and chocolate on purpose. She hadn't, of course.

Laughter wasn't appropriate. She should be devastated. Once again, the pie landed in the wrong place. Still, a stupid giggle threatened in her throat. The situation was just so... ridiculous. Did that make her terrible?

A guy's booming voice behind her made her cringe at the volume. "Oh, man. I'm sorry. I didn't see you there."

She peered over her shoulder and found Nick from Peppermint Sweet. He was out of his sweaty wear, instead in jeans and a crisp, dark blue button-down. He cleaned up well, even if he did ruin everything.

"Oh, really?" She didn't hide the snark in her voice and spun back to face Russell.

He leaned over, and the pie tin landed upright in his lap. Half the pie stayed in the tin and the other half clung to his shirt and Suzette Marie's top and arm.

"I'm so, so sorry." Her voice shook with more rising

laughter. Crap on a cracker. Why did the wrong emotion always rear its head on her? Because Chloe should feel bad about this, right? That snicker that bubbled up from her throat was disrespectful and rude. Like, really, really rude. She seemed to be the only one who saw any humor in the scenario.

Russell jumped into action. He hoisted himself and Suzette Marie up. Bits of crust fell to the floor.

Chloe swallowed and swallowed again as if that would stem the full-on snorty, tears-falling-down-her-cheeks kind of laughter that would be impossible to stop once she got started. Russell had once called it her hyena impression.

She should help make it right. "There has to be sparkling water and salt somewhere." She reached over to swipe at Suzette Marie's top with her hand towel, which hadn't left her grasp when the pie went flying.

"No." She pushed Chloe's hands away with that haughty, nasally *non* that made Chloe bolt upright in compliance. "There goes my brand new top." Suzette Marie gave off a rumbly little purr in her throat and peered down at her chest.

"It was an accident. Really." The whole idea was to look good in front of Russell—and better than Suzette Marie. She'd never launch a pie at anyone on purpose like a reality star seeking airtime.

Suzette Marie's blue eyes fired and her lips pursed.

The whole absurdity of the situation slammed into her chest. But what's done is done.

She bent down and scooped up the parts of pie that had landed on the couch with the towel. She also grabbed the tin to rescue the other half of the pie. This pie had magic to do today. Maybe Russell wouldn't mind it was a little smooshed. Plus, the clean-up job gave her something to do other than burst into a fit of giggles.

It Was All The Pie's Fault

"I'll be right back." She headed to the kitchen.

She dropped the pie pan onto the counter and the towel with the ruined parts in the sink. Okay, she could take a minute to center herself—and get the pie onto a plate to deliver to Russell. Like an apology gift.

In the other room, Suzette Marie's whine filtered through the television noise.

Chloe opened drawers and cabinets. "Salt. Salt."

Cherry juice was impossible to remove. That top was toast. She'd offer to pay for dry cleaning anyway. Chloe was fair if nothing else.

"Hey, really. I'm sorry about bumping into you like that." Nick filled the archway between the kitchen and living room. His hand slid up the wall, and he leaned against it like he was posing for a magazine or something. With his dark eyes and dark hair, he had that look that said, *"I've been good-looking my whole life, so drink it in, baby."*

She put her hands on her hips. "I'm surprised you didn't drop to your knees and start eating the pie off the floor." Her hand flew to her mouth. "I'm sorry. That was… bad."

His lips inched up. "Hand me a fork. I'll help with cleanup."

Chloe didn't have time for this. She spun in circles, glancing around at every surface. "How can someone not have salt?"

He sauntered over to the small Formica table in the corner, lifted a saltshaker and shook it at her. "This looks familiar."

She snatched it from him and turned to run smack into Russell. "Suzette Marie is asking for club soda and…" He eyed her hand. "Perfect. Salt, too." He winked and plucked it from her hand.

Her fingers curled around his arm before he could jet away. "I'm so sorry, Russell. I–I…" She twisted her mouth into a frown. This was her moment to show him how miserable she was about the pie mess, but she literally could not form words.

"Hey, don't worry." He kissed her on her cheek, which about had her knees turn to melted butter. "You just got a little enthusiastic there." The man really was wonderfulness incarnate.

"Have some pie. It solves everything." She darted to the counter and lifted the ruined treat.

He shook his head. "I should help Suzette Marie. She seems really upset." He gave a chin lift toward Nick, who'd returned to holding up the doorjamb, and then vanished.

She sighed heavily and turned back to the surviving cherry leftovers. So much pie potential wrecked. Maybe she got the mantra wrong?

She'd spent an extra amount of time pushing the Waxman Farm's organic butter— Nana's secret ingredient—into the flour. She'd also recited Nana's special mantra a thousand times along with her wish.

A huge hand fell onto her shoulder. "Chloe. Don't worry about it. You didn't mean it."

She turned to Nick. "You're right. *You* did it."

He rubbed his chin, eyes slanted down at her. Then, he chuckled and slowly shook his head.

She didn't have time for this man… this ruiner of plans. "I gotta go help."

He cocked his head toward the tin. "You mean to further mark your territory?"

Ha-ha, funny guy. Though he wasn't exactly wrong— she'd just hoped the pie would have landed in Russell's mouth. Besides, they were on a date. Or at least, were supposed to be.

She waved her hand toward him dismissively and spun away.

It Was All The Pie's Fault

In the hallway, murmured voices came from behind the bathroom door. Russell was soothing Suzette Marie. As he would be.

A giggle echoed inside. Chloe pressed her ear to the door. Clothes rustled, a groan of wood, and then Suzette Marie's voice, loud and clear.

Another soft murmur sounded. "Russell, are you sure?"

What was he doing? What was he sure about?

"Another great pie, though."

She nearly jumped out of her skin at the sound of Nick behind her. He held her pan and a fork, his cheeks bulging out.

"You really could open your own shop with this." He scooped up more of the pie and brought it to his mouth.

"I see you found a fork on your own. And no, I teach first graders. Remember?" She spluttered. Why was she bothering with this guy?

A long, female groan sounded behind the door. What the ever-loving eff? They couldn't be doing stuff, could they? In a bathroom? Of course, they could. She'd given Suzette Marie the perfect excuse to get naked and show off her *les atouts*. But she wouldn't. They were friends.

A thought crossed her mind and a gasp left her throat. Russell was making a move on her. Maybe she should knock. She raised her knuckles but stopped at the sound of a fork scraping on a tin behind her.

More smacking sounds filled the hallway. "That's a waste of talent."

She was going to have to deal with this guy, wasn't she? "Listen—"

"So, trying to get in on the action there?" He cocked his head toward the door and swallowed. "Russ sure goes for the hot ones."

43

Ouch. "Gee, thanks." She grasped the pie tin and pulled. "Give me that."

Nick clung to it and pulled it back to him. "No, I didn't mean—"

"Listen. I am on a *date*. Do you mind?"

A loud giggle sounded behind the door and Nick crossed his arms. "Oh? It's a ménage?" He set the pie pan down on the console table. "Ya know, chasing after a guy isn't the best way to land him."

She chuffed. "I'm not chasing."

Nick's dark eyes drilled down at her. "Uh-huh."

"Okay, a little chasing. But..." But what? Suzette Marie had also said to be herself, and Chloe was a doer.

Nick eyed her. "They walked in together, you know."

Something rattled in her chest like a rattlesnake tail. All the blood in her body shifted and moved like a snake's would. Russell brought Suzette Marie on *her* date? She'd agreed to it as well? No, they simply walked in together. They could have driven separately.

Yet, to be sure, her mind surfaced a fantastically brilliant idea. Chloe didn't sit around and wait for fate to deliver her life. She was a modern woman. Why should she wait for someone to notice her?

She squared herself to Nick. "Instead of standing there and acting all..." she waved her hand, "condemning because we don't really know what is unfolding here..."

Another female giggle erupted on the other side of the door. Nick raised his eyebrows. "I know what's *undressing*, though, and—"

She raised her hand to silence him. "She wouldn't. She's my friend. But you can help me." She whispered as if she needed to lower her voice. The laughter growing on the other side of the door was getting ridiculous—and loud. Her jaw clenched so hard her teeth were going to shatter. Right in her head. She'd be so toothless she couldn't eat her own pies.

"And why would I help? Russell is a player." He pointed at the bathroom door. "I'm an attorney. It would be a breach of my ethics to let you go any further with this guy with the evidence I have on him."

"It'd be a breach of ethics not to help me, Mr. Pie Thief." She moved closer to him. "Listen, I can make it worth your while. You're a Duke fan, right?"

One of his brows lifted. "Of course. They're the best team."

"I can make them win."

He made a guttural noise in his throat. "You can do that, can you?"

She didn't have time for his doubt. They were running out of time. "Yes, my pie is magic. Trust me. You ate some of it, and now, all I or you have to do is wish for them to win, and they will."

He scoffed. "Magic doesn't exist. Besides, Duke rules."

"Not today." She at least could see the score from where she stood. UNC 68, Duke 48.

A long, female murmur came through the door again. Suzette Marie even sighed in French.

"I am not talking to Russell for you."

She stomped her foot, which was silly and something her first graders would do. But jeez-Louise, he was stubborn. "Why not? You owe me. The pie launch?" She added a dash of distress to her voice because guys responded to that. At least Russell had seemed to when Suzette Marie whined about getting a little—okay, a lot—of chocolate cherry pie on her top. It had certainly made him jump into action.

He slowly shook his head.

The door cracked open. She didn't have time to negotiate.

She was going to have to put something else in motion—even non-consensually.

Chloe threw her arms around Nick, rose on her tiptoes, and went straight for his mouth. Her hands curled into his hair in case he got any ideas to run away as she kissed him.

Suzette Marie's startled, *"Oh,"* pierced the air, immediately joined by an, *"Oh, man,"* from Russell.

Playing hard to get? Check and score.

6

Soft lips. A sweet, floral scent. Warm female flesh.

His arms hadn't been around a woman too long ago, but it'd been some waif picked up at happy hour. Now, his hands held pure, soft flesh that made him want to curl his fingers deeper. Yank her closer.

Her lips slid and moved. Jesus, this woman could kiss. So, he pulled her flush against his body, bending her backward a little as he deepened the kiss.

Her chest moved against his and nearly every part of him —one part in particular—jumped to life. This was not the kiss he expected from Chloe. It was like sugar on fire.

What was he doing? He jerked backward a little. This woman was crazy. He didn't do crazy.

"Chloe?" Russell, the serial seducer, glared at him. "So. Nick Hollister. Didn't know you two were a… thing. What happened to Jeanette?"

Jesus. Russell was a piece of work. Jeanette was a woman he'd gone out with once a year and a half ago who was now married with a kid on the way, all of which Russell knew because, yeah, Russell went for her, too.

Suzette Marie's eyes darted from person to person. She shrugged and headed back to where Nick himself should be: rooting for the best NCAA Division I college basketball team.

Nick slid his hand into Chloe's, earning him one of her adorable glowers, and it nearly got him hard. This woman was no pushover, and he loved a gutsy female.

She jerked her hand free and turned back to Russell. A sugary smile he'd seen before on her rose her cheeks. "Oh, we're not—"

"Sugar, why don't we go watch the game?" He draped his arm over her shoulder and stared hard at Russell.

Chloe slipped free like his arm hadn't just encased her while she gave him one of the best kisses he'd had in... hell, ever.

In the background, both the television crowd and the guys in the room cheered.

"Yeah," Russell's hand by his side tapped his leg. "I should give Suzette Marie a ride home anyway. Looks like Bradley's a no-show, and she Ubered."

"But we were going to meet here."

Nick knew it. This was no date to Russell. Maybe a hookup if the mood struck him. The guy was the antonym of commitment.

"This was..." she waved her hand up and down toward Nick's body, "nothing."

Someone had to save this woman. Men smelled crazy a mile away, and Chloe was showing a bit too much of it today. He grasped her wandering fingers in mid-air and brought them to his lips. "Oh, I wouldn't call it nothing."

She slowly turned her head, those soft pink lips falling open in a gasp.

Russell scooted away—ostensibly to finish what he'd

started with Suzette Marie. The guy loved flavors of the week.

Chad called from the living room. "Nick, man, get your wallet out because Duke got tapped for illegal dribbling —again."

Losing a C-note in his bet with Chad? Unlikely. "Duke rules," he called out, not bothering to take his eyes off Chloe and her scowl.

"Why did you do that?" she gritted out.

That was rich. "You kissed me, Pie Queen."

"You..." she jabbed her finger in his chest, "made it epic. In front of them."

His chest puffed a little at her statement like any normal man's would at her words. "Epic, huh?"

"I was trying to show him I can play hard to get. Like Suzette Marie told me to."

"By lip-locking another guy? Yeah, jealousy *is* a decent play." He crossed his arms over his chest. "So, since I helped you, does that mean I can have the last bites of your pie?" He glanced down at the few inches of pie left in the tin, which should not go to waste.

"No." She grasped the pie tin. "No magic for you. You have to help me fix this."

How was this woman walking around unattended? Unsupervised? "I fixed your future." Getting her away from Russell? Consider it his good deed of the day. "And magic doesn't exist."

Her lips twisted and he just could not stop staring at them. "You ate some of it, and now, all you have to do is wish for Duke to win, and they will. That means you owe me because now things are better for you and even worse for me."

Eyes back to hers, he drank in her sweet face. "Things are

now better for you. Trust me. And Duke will pull it out on their own."

She smirked. "The score is now UNC 72, Duke 64."

"In basketball, it isn't over until the last second."

Chad's loud laughter cut through the air. "Caught traveling now. Get ready to hand over your money, Hollister. A second hundred to me given the spread."

Damn him. He should never have let the guy goad him into spicing up the bet that way.

"Oh, bet on the spread, too? I also can wish…" she lifted a fork and took a delicate bite of cherry pie, "for them to lose—spectacularly."

While she slowly chewed, they stared at one another like an old Western movie stand-off.

"Why Russell?" Being hell-bent on a guy like Russell made no sense.

What Nick had seen of the guy on the basketball court on Sundays when he spared an hour to get some exercise in was all he needed to know. The guy did not like to lose, and he had a different girl showing up at the court every other weekend. The French bombshell would be gone soon enough. Someone else would interest him.

"Because he's perfect for me. Please." Her shoulders drooped. "Help me fix this."

Chad appeared in the doorway. "Got your money out?"

Nick raised his hand. "Be there in a second" He then turned back to Chloe. Her eyes had grown watery. Shit.

Okay, this Chloe Hart might be a little mad—and she had terrible taste in men—but she didn't deserve to be humiliated by Russell. He himself wasn't exactly the best judge of what worked or not in romance land. And nothing pulled him in faster than helping an underdog.

"Okay." He crossed his arms. "Dazzle me with this magic."

It Was All The Pie's Fault

He raised one hand in a stop sign gesture. "I don't believe it, but I'm not about to lose my C-note to Chad there."

"Or several," she added.

Whatever. "And I do owe you for the pie... thing."

"The ruination of my future."

This woman truly had never been out of this little town, had she? "Hey, may I remind you I may have helped you launch a pie, but you launched yourself at me. I'd say you helped with this *ruination*."

"I did that for a singular purpose."

He sighed heavily. As an attorney, he knew when to stop arguing. "I can help you with Russell." He didn't know how, but he'd figure something out.

Her smile returned. She set the pie down, smoothed down her cherry print skirt—which he was totally digging—and took in a deep breath.

"I wish for Duke to win today."

"Spectacularly?"

Her grin widened. "Spectacularly. And done."

"That was it?"

She lifted one shoulder and cocked her head. "The pie cannot be denied."

Cute. He huffed out a half-laugh. "Okay, let's watch Duke win and make Russell jealous some more."

She stopped short. "No. No more you and I together stuff. It's lying."

"It's strategic."

"It's dishonest." She put her hands on her hips.

"Like your kiss was?"

She dropped her hands to her sides. "That was a mistake." She shook her head as if attempting to shake the memory of it even though no one moved their lips like that and didn't enjoy it. She then tried to slide by him but stopped short.

Russell had returned to the hallway with Suzette Marie. They glided out the door without so much as a goodbye.

Good riddance. He turned to Chloe, whose eyes, round and misty, stared hard at the door.

The guys in the other room roared again.

"Hey man, your effing Duke tied up the game," Chad shouted.

He got himself in view of the screen just in time to see a slam dunk that made the rest of the team jump up and down.

Chad shook his head. "Holy shit."

Another basket. Then another.

"Looks like the greatest basketball team in the NCAA is banging them out." Nick cocked his head toward Chad. "Get your money out."

Chad cursed, and Chloe, now standing in the archway, peered at him with a watery smile on her face.

Nick stared at the television. *Chloe did not make that happen.* He glanced her way. She still stared at the door, and her bottom lip quivered.

Oh, man. Nothing turned him impotent faster than tears. Before he could shake their effect, she yanked open the door handle.

"Hey, Chloe. You okay?" He grabbed her coat. Before he could catch up, though, she was through the door. If she ran after Russell…

He got to the doorway, and wow, she could move. She was down the sidewalk in seconds. He followed, but she was inside a Honda Civic with all the windows rolled up before he could reach her.

He ducked down and peered in the window. "Seriously. You alright?"

Given the waterfall cascading down her cheeks, no, she wasn't alright. She started up her car, and the hood fell away under his hand as she sped off.

He should be glad to be rid of the crazy aura. Still, he felt like shit for her. No woman should shed tears over Russell Langston.

He lifted her coat in his hands and, for reasons he couldn't fathom, he ambled to his car and threw it in the front seat. He'd get it back to her—and shake some sense into the woman—if he could. The woman believed in magic. Who else knew what rattled around in that pretty head of hers?

7

Nick stared at the tinfoil triangle on his desk that contained the last three bits of Chloe's cherry pie and shook his head. The girl truly could bake—and kiss. Two things he should not still be thinking about.

He twirled the pie package on his desk. *Magic pie. What a crock.* But he wouldn't mind another taste of her lips.

Fat chance of that happening again, though. The girl had cried over Russell Langston, of all people. Shit, he felt bad about her tears even if she was delusional about men and magic.

Shake it off, man. He had enough on his plate and couldn't worry about a woman who'd goaded him into some jealousy scheme. If he didn't get a call back in five minutes from Jack Trainer, opposing counsel on the Fernandez case, he was in some *real* shit. The Weeks, Shipman, and Carter law firm did not like to lose.

He opened up the tinfoil. *What the hell?* He took the last bite of pie. "I wish that Johnson and Sons would forfeit and give my client a dream settlement." He swallowed. A rap on his doorframe sounded.

"That work?" His colleague, John Hammond, filled the doorway.

He stood and stretched his back. "If only. Back from the courthouse?"

"Restraining order renewed." John waved the papers in his hand.

Nick lifted his chin. "Let me see." He still couldn't believe his sister Daphne had waited this long to tell him her loser second husband had been regularly beating the shit out of her since their wedding last year.

John dropped the papers into his hand and tumbled into the chair in front of his desk. "Didn't take you for a brown bag lunch guy."

Nick eyed the paperwork, only half-listening to John. "What? Oh, the pie. Yeah, it's from some girl who brought it to Chad's shindig." The softness of her lips rose in his mind again.

"Hey, can't believe Duke pulled out a win at the last minute yesterday. Didn't see that one coming given their shitty season."

Basketball was a better topic for his brain to settle on than imagining Chloe Hart's kissing skills. "Neither did I." And pie had nothing to do with it. They were a great team, period. Still, he wasn't throwing out some of the best dessert he'd ever eaten. "I should have been here handling the McPherson case." He balled up the tinfoil and tossed it into the trashcan.

"Sorry, man. It must be agony to not work seven days a week anymore."

"Making partner only happens one way. Work." Even if his partners said they didn't want to see him in the office on Saturdays anymore, he couldn't give up his schedule. His cases weren't going to win themselves, and he hadn't been having too many wins lately.

"You're in luck. This afternoon, we're free of Johnson Construction popping in with more of their bullshit. Apparently, the lead on their side is out sick."

Jesus, no wonder the guy was ignoring his calls. It was probably a stall technique. They likely wanted more time and were planning something, which meant he needed to, as well. At least he now had an afternoon free to get ready for whatever "it" was.

"So, what's her name?"

His mind spun from the sudden change in topic. "Who?"

"The chick getting all domestic on you. The pie?" His eyes glanced down at the trashcan by his desk.

He waved his hand dismissively. "No one. Just a random girl who was throwing herself at Russell Langston, of all people." Talk about wasting some fantastic kissing skills.

"Langston? The guy with the subscription to the hottie of the week?"

"Yeah. He and his hottie du jour got a pie dumped on them by her. That was…" he pointed to the trash, "what was left."

John laughed. "Epic. So glad I'm married and don't have to put up with that crazy chick stuff anymore."

"Chloe's not crazy." He'd thought so yesterday, but this morning woke up with her lips on his brain. The memory refused to be shaken. One other thought, too. She was lost—and naïve as hell.

Her weepy hazel eyes rose in his mind. *Shit*. He scrubbed his hair.

John quirked a smile. "Chloe, huh? So, you do know her name."

"Yeah." Of course, he did. He stretched his back. "Got work to do. And you do, too."

"Yeah, well, give the pie maker some flowers. Gets me laid by my wife every time."

It Was All The Pie's Fault

"I don't have time for women." *Or being occupied with how a woman kisses, wondering what else she could do with that mouth.*

"That's a shame." Hank Carter appeared like an apparition in his doorway. One second he wasn't there, the next he was.

"Oh, he's got a girl, alright. Made him some pie." John grinned at him.

Nick was going to kill him.

Hank stepped in deeper. "Glad to hear it. Relationships are a part of a well-rounded life."

Weeks, Shipman, and Carter just had to bring in that life coach consultant who declared their workplace toxic to human health. So much organizational development bullshit.

John's lips inched up further. "Yeah, Nick here's enamored with a baker."

What was it about married people wanting everyone else to take the wedded death march with them—including the partners of WSC?

Hank knocked on the doorjamb. "Good, because all work and no play makes for dull partners." He then ghosted away.

John and Nick exchanged glances.

John grinned. "You're getting it alright."

"I'll believe it when I get the signing agreement."

John stood and stretched. "Yeah, but let me give you a word of advice. Bring the baking chick to the wine and cheese on Friday. Hank'll love that."

"I hate that thing."

"Overheard Hannity saying he'd love a shot at the L.A. office."

"You lying to me?"

"Nope. So, show Hank you're not wanting to go there to chase Hollywood babes." John waggled his eyebrows. "Show him you're stable."

He could see that given how conservative Hank appeared. "I am stable." *It's marriage that knocked people off*

57

their rocker. Look at his sister, still believing her ex might change.

But a date to the "whine and cheese" as he'd often thought of it? His partners had suggested he enjoy some extracurricular activity, and what better way than with a woman who would never fall in love with him because her attentions lay elsewhere? He liked her well enough. She had spunk even if she believed in magic pie.

As soon as John left, Nick opened his browser and Googled her name and "elementary school." Chloe had said first graders, right?

"There you are, Chloe Hart. Broadstreet Elementary." Her face shone from the screen, sporting a radiant smile.

He grabbed his coat. He had another coat to deliver to one crazy pie queen—and a deal to propose.

8

"Amy, sit down, please." All morning, the little girl had not been able to still her body for five minutes.

"But Cameron took my crayon!" The girl's plaid skirt flounced as she thunked herself down onto her desk chair. She crossed her arms and dropped her head down in pure protest.

"We're sharing, remember?" Chloe's teaching aide, Katie, bent down toward her and placed her hand on the little girl's back to soothe her. Amy was known for full-on meltdowns over art supplies.

The girl lifted her head, her eyes dropped in half-mast. "But it's my turn." Her little six-year-old head theatrically dropped back to her arms.

And Chloe had thought yesterday was dramatic. Nothing compared to a classroom full of first graders.

However, she'd learned something from this past weekend. She wouldn't try to deliver a cherry pie again because clearly, someone upstairs—*Sorry, Nana*—objected to her using the special recipe. Reason? Unknown, but she'd not try it again. Not without a sign. Like a *billboard*.

Rather, she made a pineapple-mango pie and left it in Russell's school box along with an appropriately sappy apology note. Pineapples symbolized welcome and warmth (oh, please let Russell welcome her back into his good graces), and mangos symbolized love and happiness (oh please, *please*, Universe, let Russell fall for her like a soufflé).

She had to try *something*. She wasn't one to give up.

She'd also left a gift certificate to L'Orangerie boutique for Suzette Marie to get a new top—one that would lure a man who was not Russell.

That last part couldn't be too hard. Not by the way Mr. Markinson, their principal, eyed her as she sauntered by in the hallway this morning—and Suzette Marie responded with a slow wink. Then again, she winked at every male her eyes landed upon.

The woman couldn't help herself, could she? She flirted so easily, so effortlessly Chloe had begun to believe Suzette Marie didn't even realize it was seductive. Maybe she could learn a thing or two from the woman.

Chloe clapped her hands. "Okay, everyone, time to put your art projects away. It's time for a story."

A rap against the glass on her door sounded. Nick the Pie Destroyer's face beamed at her from the hallway. He held up an enormous bouquet of peonies and white daisies and grinned through the glass.

"Hey, Katie, give me a sec."

"Sure thing. Cameron, Cameron. Put your lunch back. It's not time."

Chloe cracked open the door and flowers attacked her face.

"I came to see how you are," Nick's rumbly voice said behind the blooms.

She pushed the petals from her face. "Oh? How did you get past the front desk?"

It Was All The Pie's Fault

"There's a front desk?"

She took the bouquet more to hold off an incoming sneeze than anything else since he kept thrusting them at her. "Don't tell me you bypassed all the security and just peered into every classroom until you found mine."

"I figured you needed this." He held out the coat she'd abandoned at the basketball party.

She took it and the flowers. "Thanks."

"And I need to talk with you. Got a sec?"

"Miss Hart. Miss Hart." A tiny hand was yanking at her skirt.

She grasped Amy's little hand with her free one. Before Chloe could muster a protest, Nick darted inside the door.

"Oh, no, you can't—"

"Are you Miss Hart's boyfriend?" the little girl asked with a level of enthusiasm usually reserved for cookie breaks.

Chloe should have ordered Nick to leave immediately, but three of her other little girls, Maribelle, Tessa, and Bailey, surrounded him. Nick towered over their little bodies.

"No. I've been told we're nothing." He inclined his head in mock despair toward the rest of the class, who suddenly had much interest in this interloper.

Amy held up a palm. "Why not? Miss Hart is nice, and she smells good."

"She does. Nick Hollister, at your service, ladies." He slapped his hand to his chest and bowed.

"He's handsome. Not as much as my daddy, but his shoes are good." Maribelle pointed toward Nick's feet.

Amy's mouth dropped open, and she dramatically peered over at Nick's loafers. "They're shiny."

Maribelle shrugged delicately. "Daddy says shoes are important."

"Oooh." Amy absorbed this wisdom.

"Girls." Chloe steered Amy and Maribelle away from

Nick. "Back to your seats. Mr. Hollister is a friend and has to go back to wherever he came from." She glared at him. "Isn't that right, Mr. Hollister?"

She set the flowers and her coat down on her desk and clapped her hands. "No storytime unless everyone is sitting in their places. You listen to Miss Katie, now." She turned to Nick. "Really, I have to get back, and you do, too."

"One second? I won't take long."

She took his arm and led him toward the door. "Sorry, I don't have time. And you are violating school policy. You shouldn't be running through the hallways."

She closed the door behind them and glanced up and down the hallway. In about ten seconds, her students would overrun Katie inside. Who could she get to escort Nick out?

He stared down at her. "I didn't mean to intrude. I wanted to check on you. I mean, you seemed really upset yesterday, and I apologize again about the pie—"

She waved him silent. "At least no one will forget it. And thank you again for… the jealousy attempt."

"That's the first time a woman has thanked me for making her cry."

Yes, humiliating. "I don't usually act like that."

His eyes glittered in amusement under the fluorescent lights. "Kiss someone you don't know?"

"Cry." Why was she even having this conversation with him? He needed to go.

"Then you would be the most unusual woman I've ever met."

"You make them cry often, I suppose."

He stepped closer. "I try to avoid it."

"Listen…" She jerked her thumb toward her classroom door. "There will be a coup in less than two minutes if I don't get back. You have to leave."

In her periphery, she saw Russell's classroom door crack

It Was All The Pie's Fault

open. He stepped out. His deep, wonderful voice rang out as he faced into his classroom. "Listen to Miss Davidson. I'll be right back."

Oh, maybe he was coming to see her to thank her for the pineapple-mango pie.

Nick cleared his throat. He stared down at her with yet another amused grin on his face. "Quit mooning in his direction."

"Mooning? I do not *moon*." She glared at Nick, refusing to dignify his ridiculous assertion with a response.

Nick ran a hand down his chin. "You deserve better than Russell."

Like this man knew anything about him. "Oh, I deserve him, alright." Dang it, Russell was moving down the hallway away from her.

Nick placed a hand on the lockers behind her and leaned over, which sent her back against the cold metal doors. "The question is does he deserve *you*?"

What? She and Russell were made for each other. He'd merely been waylaid by Suzette Marie's obvious charms. She pushed on Nick's pecs to remove him from her personal space. Wow, solid. He had quite the chest under that smooth cotton shirt.

Nick's eyes lasered down on her. "So, kiss me again."

Was this man on drugs? "Are you crazy—"

"So he can see. Hey, Russ," Nick called. Russell looked back at them. Nick reached down and brought his lips so close his breath warmed her cheek. "Trust me." He pressed a kiss to her forehead. "Now really kiss me. Like yesterday." His dark eyes held a dare.

She wasn't that easy. She would be for Russell but not this guy. "You wish." She glanced at Russell, who had paused at least, but then sauntered away like he hadn't seen another man put his lips on her for the second time.

Nick dropped his head to stare down at his shiny shoes and chuckled.

"*Great.*" Her hiss slithered through the now-empty hallway. "You did that to one-up him, didn't you?" She pushed at him, but he barely moved. He was too big, and *bossy*, and seemingly hell-bent on wrecking her life.

His amused snicker erupted once more. "I helped you."

"How? Now he thinks I'm really *with* you." Or *still* with him since she'd engineered a fake something-or-other with a guy she was, quite frankly, disliking with a vengeance. She ducked under his arm.

Nick dropped his arms to his side and stuffed his hands into his trouser pockets. "To make him jealous, of course."

Men. "What century are you from? Clearly, he doesn't get that way. He's—"

"A *guy*. He wants to keep his options open. Trust me. I know." He leaned forward. A curl fell across his forehead.

She crossed her arms. "You know how to lure men? You do it often?"

"You really are cute," he chortled.

So was he. Well, not cute, more like classically handsome, which only made him worse—kinda like the devil. The devil would be good-looking and seductive and steal futures. This guy did this often, didn't he? Crash in and move that colossal body around like he owned the place.

"Chloe, why do you want to be with this guy so badly? You have yet to give me a good answer." What a silly question. He raised his hand—probably because she gave him a death stare in response. "Actually, never mind. None of my business. You can tell me about it over dinner on Friday. I have a proposition for you."

"No way. I don't cheat."

"You can't cheat if you're single. And you know, most women would consider me a catch."

It Was All The Pie's Fault

She rolled her eyes. "Come *on*. No, thank you. Now, I have to get back inside, or the natives will be climbing the walls. You'll go straight out, right? I mean, you're not a danger—"

"I'm an attorney."

She cocked her head. "Is that supposed to make me feel better or something?"

"Yes, actually. And my offer stands if you change your mind."

"I won't."

He slowly shook his head. "Alright, I'm going. And don't worry. I'll head straight to my car and won't lure any little children with candy." He turned and chuckled. "By the way, Duke won."

"Of course they did." She strode inside without looking back at the man.

"Coincidence," he called.

The door clicked shut and left him standing in the hallway alone.

Whatever, God's gift to womankind. She wouldn't see him again, but that was fine by her. Now she had to revise her day's wishing—or add to it. First, she needed Russell to get she was not interested in Nick. Two, she needed him to erase the memory of Nick putting his lips on her.

Given the last few days? She'd think the Universe would give her a twofer.

9

Chloe rocked that school librarian look. The prim clip of her voice was oddly attractive. Winning this woman would be a challenge—except for Russell, who could probably make this woman his slave. This did not sit well with Nick. Plus, her understanding of men could fit into a teaspoon.

As luck would have it, he ran into Russell in the parking lot. His gaze was locked on Suzette Marie lecturing some students under a tree across the parking lot. She was pointing to various things and reciting French names.

"Tree. *L'arbre*. Sky. *Ciel.*"

The woman was a knockout. She'd had all the guys at Chad's football party drooling, for sure. He, however, never went for that twig look. Any woman he could crush with the first embrace was off the table for him.

He and Russell exchanged handshakes.

Nick stared down at the guy. "Hey, sorry to hear about UNC."

"Yeah. Strange game, huh?" Russell's weak chin waggled. Nick did not get what Chloe saw in him.

It Was All The Pie's Fault

"You and Suzette Marie, too…"

"Yeah, trying. She's something." He then flushed. Man, the guy was pussy *fouetté*. Russell was into this Suzette Marie chick. Chloe needed to move on.

"So, what are you doing here? Got a kid enrolled?" Russell's forehead wrinkled like he was trying to figure out how Nick was standing in an elementary school parking lot. Nick didn't get it either now that he stood there.

What the hell. He'd see how the guy reacted to the truth. "I came by to see Chloe Hart. The girl's got some…" he cocked his head "baking skills."

Russ shrugged. "Yeah, I guess."

He didn't know? Nick thought for sure Chloe would have held him down and force-fed him some of her pie given how much she believed it worked magic. "So, you two ever…"

"We had a few moments. She's… sweet." He nearly patted her head with his words as if he was talking about a cute but bothersome puppy.

"She's got some sass, that's for sure." Her glare when he suggested they go out was fun. She could fry an egg with those hazel eyes.

Russell's spine straightened a bit. "So, you came by to see her."

A challenge swam in the guy's eyes. Nick's interest in Chloe wasn't welcomed. As he'd thought—Russell wanted both women's attention.

"Listen, gotta go." Russell turned away but spun backward and gave him a gun finger. "Hoops Saturday, right?"

"Right." Part of his get-a-life program included stopping by for an hour of basketball before heading to the office. He could shower at WSC—he had many times. He had more clothes at the office than he had at home at this point.

As he watched Russell saunter away, Russell's attitude

toward Chloe tugged at his chest. The guy knew nothing about the woman who was obsessed with him, but he sure as shit was enjoying it. Nick might have to do something about Chloe's situation even if the woman herself didn't.

10

Chloe was late as hell. Thanks to a sleepless night, she'd gotten a late start to Peppermint Sweet. Greta and Scarlett must be wondering where the heck their Saturday morning pies were.

She balanced the three pie boxes in her arms and shut her car door with her foot. Thunderclouds rumbled overhead. She'd have to run.

Pounding on pie pastry last night had turned out to be a good way to get out frustrations. Frustrations about things like how Dolores at the front desk had spilled some gossip about Russell and Suzette Marie, about how Russell was trying to go to France with Suzette Marie on her student school trip. Never mind he hated flying and taught American history for God's sake.

Chloe jogged around the corner, her purse strap barely staying on her shoulder, and slammed into a wall. A cry flew out of her throat as she stumbled backward. A powerful set of arms caught her before she landed on her butt.

White shirt, blue suit. She looked up. It was Nick.

"Whoa, it's the pie queen." He smiled down at her.

Bright purple stains spread over his wide chest.

"Oh, no." The three paper boxes holding the pies had flattened between them.

He reached down and scooped up some of the pie half-hanging off the edge of the box. He brought it to his lips. "Mmmm. You really are a talented baker."

"You just ate pie off your shirt." She stepped back again and let the top box fall to the ground. She managed to keep the other two boxes—totally mashed—in her arms.

He sucked on the end of his thumb. "Five-second rule. Pie's still good." He then reached down to the ground and broke off a larger piece from inside the box.

"What are you doing? That is on the *ground*."

The Neanderthal rose and pointed a finger at her. "Technically, it was still in the box." He shoved a sizeable piece in his mouth. His eyes rolled back and his head dropped back. "Mmm. A-mazing."

"You. Are. A. Savage."

His eyes sparkled. "I've been called worse." If pride had a physical form, it was now rolling off him in waves.

Chloe wasn't a violent person. No, indeed. But right now, punching one smug attorney with blueberry stains on his shirt—and now his teeth—would feel *sooo* good. "I was trying to sell those, you know."

He shrugged and reached into his back pocket with his blueberry-stained fingers. "How much? I'll take all three."

She stepped backward and clutched her two remaining, totally smushed pie boxes. "You will *not*."

A woman with her hand hooked into a man's arm scooted by them. Their faces said everything: *"Let's leave the crazy people be."*

"So, they're not for sale?" Nick shook his head. "Look. My fault. I'm trying to do the right thing here."

There was nothing right about any of this. But he had eaten it, so she could wish him away, right?

Nana had specifically marked the blueberry-lavender pie as "for emergencies only." It basically made everything right again. Blueberries symbolized protection, and lavender represented purity, grace, and calmness. Her life was most definitely in an emergency. First, Russell making moon eyes at Suzette Marie, and now, this guy constantly showing up?

She reached down and picked a small piece up and stuck it in her mouth. She glared at him as she mantra-ed her way to Nick Hollister freedom.

I wish for you to find true love.

I wish for you to find the woman of your dreams.

I wish for you to go off and spend allll your time with that poor wretched woman.

There. She even remembered to make it a positive set of wishes, one of Nana's golden rules.

I wish for you to leave this town and make your dreams come true.

He chuckled. "See? Still good."

Then he drew closer. Everything about him was big—too big, like the Hulk about to smash her plans. He had that wicked glint in his eye she didn't trust—like he was going for more of her pie.

"What did I eat? It was fantastic."

She tried to scoot by him. "Blueberry-lavender."

He grasped her arm. "Let me guess. It's magic."

She spun back to him and stepped closer. "Go on. Make fun all you want. It matters not to me."

The man had the gall to smirk down at her. "Chloe, let's go inside. Talk about my proposition."

Could the guy not take a hint? "With you? No." She tossed her chin upward to make her point. "I'd rather go out with a German shepherd than you." At least dogs were loyal.

"I get that. But would you like to hear what would work with Russell?"

"I know what will work." She had to get Russell to eat her frackin' pie—and not off the ground.

"No, you don't." He inclined his head toward Peppermint Sweet. "It's just coffee. Or tea, if you prefer. If you want to know what will work with Russell, you'll hear me out."

He took the two ruined pie boxes from her, and somehow, she found herself sitting inside Peppermint Sweet—only with the wrong guy.

～

Nick commandeered the little bistro table at the front window. The tiny little chair barely fit him, but Chloe seemed to have an affinity for the spot—something about the silly hearts scrolled into the backs of the chairs, if memory served. Plus, the seats had the best view of Brickman Park across the street where the giant, historic maple tree sat in its center. Funny how he'd never really looked at this place before even though he'd driven down this street a hundred times.

He bought himself a coffee and her tea. "How long have you been baking for this place?"

"About a year. And only when I have time. Greta is good that way." She picked up the ceramic mug with the red rim around its bowl and blew on the rising steam.

Such a casual tone. This woman really had no idea the repeat customer base she was helping the shop owner build. "I've come back a few times. I'm surprised I haven't run into you here."

"I don't have much time to hang around. But Peppermint Sweet's coffee is the best in town."

"So's your pie." He inclined his chin to the leftover pie

It Was All The Pie's Fault

she'd secured in the extra chair next to her. After he'd paid for all three of the pies, Scarlett saved one piece of the blueberry-lavender. Chloe had commandeered it, and he had bargained hard for access to it—and lost. Chloe made most of the opposing counsels he'd faced look like kittens.

"In fact, this coffee would go well with that leftover piece."

Her pink lips pursed once more as she blew a light breath over her drink. "I'm sure it would. You can buy some..." she glanced over at the glass display case, "oh, darn." She settled her hazel eyes back on him. "They were ruined by a human wall."

She had spunk in spades. "So, I'm human now?"

She harumphed.

So, he wasn't getting any more of her *magic*. Fine by him. He could live without more sugar. He could not live with her constant delusions around a man who went through women as fast as water over Niagara Falls.

What was it about women and their poor choices around men? His mother, his sister, and now this lost first grade teacher who believed wishing made things so.

Even if Suzette Marie had pussy-whipped Russell for a bit, the man was never marrying her *or* Chloe. And twice now, the man had shown such little interest in Chloe that Nick was getting offended on her behalf.

"I'm glad you chose this spot, though." She smoothed down her khaki pants and crossed her legs. She stared out at the park. "I've always loved that maple tree."

He took a gulp of the scalding coffee. "Looks old. Probably seen a lot."

"This is where Russell and I first met—even before I went to work for Broadstreet. It was here I learned the school was hiring before it even was posted, and that we both come from founding families of Moorsville. Did you know that fifteen families gathered here under that tree and decided to start this town?"

He squinted his eyes at the tree as if that would raise up a historic scene. "That right?" He could almost see it.

"Yep. That tree is magic." She pulled one leg up under her and faced him.

What was up with all this airy-fairy stuff? "You do believe in your voodoo."

"It's *magic*, and belief is powerful. So, now, Mr. Attorney, since you keep showing up, I'm taking it as a sign. How are you going to help me? I'm dying to know what you have in mind."

"I figured you were a girl who didn't like mystery. You're a planner."

She dropped her chin and looked at him from under her lashes. "I teach first graders. Plans are for the new teachers who just got out of school. I go with the flow."

"Or you like to organize chaos. Which is exactly what romantic entanglements bring." And even greater disasters.

"So cynical, Nick Hollister."

"Realistic."

"Don't believe in love?" She lifted her cup.

"I believe in work. So, before I tell you how I can help you, tell me something—why do you believe your pies are magic?"

"I don't just believe. I know." She took a delicate sip of her tea. She had small hands, smooth.

"Care to support that premise with evidence?"

She set her cup down and sighed heavily. "History. I've seen it work all my life. I learned to bake when I was a first grader."

"Like your students' age? Isn't that a little young?" As if he could remember what being six years old was like.

"People have so little faith in the young. They're sponges.

It Was All The Pie's Fault

They're absorbing everything at that age. My Nana, after she took me in when my parents died, thought it might help. She was the one who showed me the magic." She shrugged.

Shit, a pang went off him. He'd lost his parents young, as well. "Did it help?"

"It did." She sucked in a long breath. "But I waited until I was twelve first to test the power, to see if I, like my Nana, had the touch. It was an apple and cinnamon pie that I gave to my math teacher before a test. I suck at math but I aced it."

"Did you study?"

"Of course. But I'd studied before, and it didn't help. Then, there was the banana coconut cream. Jeffrey won our high school championship—he was the quarterback—and he asked me to the prom when I told him about the wish I made around that." She snapped her fingers. "Oh, and the pistachio mint cream got me into Broadstreet Elementary school."

"Pie did all that, huh?"

"Yep. Two dozen others were up for the job, but I showed up to the recruiter meeting with a little pastry insurance. She hadn't had lunch. Guess what she had instead?" She sang that last part.

"Pistachio mint cream."

"And look at me now. In the best school system in the state. I'd also wished that I'd meet the love of my life through this job. Someone who'd want to settle down with me here in Moorsville."

"And you think the pie brought you to Russell."

"I did until that *French toothpick* arrived and things went haywire." She threw herself against the back of her chair and crossed her arms.

He chuckled a little but sobered immediately. She thought so little of herself. "Never occurred to you that you got all those things in the past on your own merit?"

"Maybe. But the pie makes it so."

75

Man, he really could go for some pie right now. "Does it matter what kind?"

"Not really. But I do like to match up the symbolism of the ingredients with the intention. It gives it extra *oomph* when I do that."

The woman had some dedication to her spellwork or whatever it was she did. He'd give her that. "So, bake yourself another pie and wish Russell right into your bed."

She mock-punched his arm. "You are such a man. Do all men focus on nothing but smutty times?"

"*Smutty times?* Yes."

She straightened her scarf. "At least you're honest."

"I'm an attorney, remember? We are bound to the truth."

"So. Truth. It doesn't work unless the other person eats it. Then, I have to make the wish—or they can—and it has to be something they wouldn't object to outright. It can be for me or them, but it works best when it's for both."

"Ah, so that's why you keep showing up with pie. To make Russell eat it. But he's not... biting?"

"Ha-ha." She lifted her tea and took a long swallow.

"But what if Russell would object to your wish? What if he didn't want to die in this town? Your idea of happy ever after wasn't good for him?" *Or you.*

Her mouth dropped to an "O." "Who would object to love? And what is wrong with this town? It's wonderful."

Moorsville was okay if you were into picturesque Hallmark scenes. But he certainly wasn't dying here. He'd be on a plane to Los Angeles in a few months. "You should become an attorney." She knew how to twist things, for sure.

"No, thank you. Now, how are you going to help me make things right?"

If he made things right, she wouldn't be interested in the guy. Russell just wanted to win the latest shiny girl. She'd learn, and with his plan, she'd learn faster than she might on her own. "I can help you with Russell if you help me."

She cocked her head. "How?"

"I need a date for a few company functions. Come with me, and I will show you exactly how to get Russell back." His partners needed to see him with a woman, so here—a woman. A pretty one, too. Not in an obvious Suzette Marie-way, who looked like any other model from a perfume ad but a real woman.

Chloe smiled easily, and her eyes danced with her thoughts. She laughed. "A date? I'd think *a catch* like you would have women all over them."

True, a woman hadn't turned him down since high school. But then, he hadn't asked a woman out in years and only engaged in mutually-agreed-upon hookups when the urge struck. "That's not the issue."

Her cute little dent between her eyes formed. "Then why me?"

"You're in love with someone else. It makes you perfect. No strings. I'm trying to make partner this year, and management likes its senior counsel... well-rounded."

She huffed a little and took another sip of her tea. "You need a token female to impress your bosses. Got it. But if I agree to this, there will be no 'real girlfriend' shenanigans."

"Shenanigans?" Her serious tone made him chuckle.

She squared herself to him. "In other words, no more attempted kissing, no luring me to your man cave. Capisce?"

The girl made him laugh, that was for sure. "Promise."

"Okay, now, about Russell... spill."

He let out a long sigh and rested his elbows on the table. "First, you need to understand where you're starting from. Here's my assessment of your situation."

She smoothed down her khakis again. "I'm listening."

"You've got two problems going around Russell

Langston." He took in her cardigan sweater and those beige pants. As much as she rocked the prim lady look, he knew enough about Russell to know she'd have to upscale her wardrobe. The man was as shallow as a fish when it came to how women looked.

"Only two problems?" She rolled her eyes. "I can name one and it starts with the letter S."

"Suzette Marie is the least of your worries." This woman was fighting the wrong dragon. "I have a hunch you're going to keep trying things with Russell, and it's going to get you in trouble. He could sue for workplace harassment. Or get a restraining order."

She sat up straight. "He wouldn't."

"You wouldn't believe what I've seen happen by people who 'wouldn't.' So, I'm going to help you even though you deserve better. He only wants who everyone else wants and—"

"If you're here to talk me out of Russell—"

"I'm not, but don't be surprised if after I help you, you don't want him after all."

She scoffed. "That will never happen."

This woman might be truly delusional. "If my suspicions are true and Russell does indeed just want to win—"

"Which I don't believe he does."

He folded his arms over his chest. "But if I'm right, you walk away."

"If what you said is true, then yes, I would. But he's *not*, so I *won't*. You're wrong about him."

"I'm not." He eyed the pie on the chair next to her. "But there's more."

"Go on."

"I'd think better with some of your pie."

She gave him a half-smile. "Of course, you would." She

reached over, undid the tinfoil, and handed him a fork. "There's only one piece left anyway."

He lit into the pie and nearly swooned. Man, he really needed to have this every day. "You need to understand there is a trick..." Nick took another huge mouthful of pie and held up one finger until he could swallow, "to any negotiation—"

"We aren't in a negotiation. We're in a rescue. Russell has an infatuation. Merely sidetracked." She ran her finger along her mug rim. "I mean, how do I go from being *amazing* and *I'm so glad you're here* and *you're the type of woman a man falls for*—yes, his exact words to me—to that... that..."

"French bombshell? Easy. She's hot as fuck. And she makes him feel like he won the lottery."

Okay, his statements were harsh and they landed like a bomb by the way her eyes widened. But they were the truth.

"Gee, thanks."

"It's not you. He's a guy." The worst kind. The kind that said those forever bullshit words to a woman like Chloe, probably knowing full well the effect they'd have. Women like her had one speed—dead run to the marital coffin.

Plus, words mattered. As an attorney, he would know.

He took a sip of coffee, which was amazing. "Whatever you want to call what we're doing here, you're going to need to first recognize your *hostage* situation."

She made a very unladylike harrumph noise. "I'm not—"

"Yes, you are. He's got you by the balls... proverbially speaking. The trick to any successful takeover—"

"*Rescue.*"

He sighed and then measured his next words carefully. "The *trick* is not to get him to cave but to get him to desperately want—preferably *need*—what you have. Then, you make it difficult for him to get it." He pointed at her. "Unless he pleases you."

"He pleases me. And you sound like Suzette Marie. She sort of said the same thing."

"You should listen to us. He has no doubts about the fact that you want him. *That* is a mistake. Groveling with your pies." He gestured down to the nearly-empty tin.

Now she was getting pissed off. Her eyes fired a golden light. "I don't grovel. I offer. I'm generous."

"You're too generous. He's had too much power over you. You're always there for him." He waved his fork. "What's he got to work for? Suzette Marie makes men win her, doesn't she?"

"This is the part where you tell me men are simple creatures. Smutty times. Scoring a touchdown. *Winning*." She cocked her head at each word.

"Yes. You need to treat yourself like a prize. Because you are."

Her face stilled. "And then he'll be mine?"

"If you want him... though I'll never understand why."

"I thought you two were friends."

"We play basketball once a week. How he plays hoops is all I need to know about the man. We are *not* friends." He scraped his fork along the bottom of the pie tin and brought the final remains to his mouth.

"So, what do I need to do?"

He swallowed. "I'll explain it over dinner. Friday night. Our first date. And, as part of our deal, I'd like you to supply me with pie, too."

A half-smile formed on her face. "So, you believe in my magic."

"Russell needs to see you making them for someone else. Make sure he learns of it." Whatever made Duke win was pure skill on the team's part, but it seemed important to her that her pies were magical. Who was he to disabuse her of what got her through the day? Plus, he liked her, and they

It Was All The Pie's Fault

could help each other. She wanted Russell. He wanted to make partnership—preferably one that got him out of this tiny town. He'd also get his sister to move with him, far away from her ex. Double win.

"I get it," she sniffed. "The pies will add to the illusion of my completely made-up interest in you."

There went that schoolmarm voice again. She had no idea how alluring that was, did she?

He grabbed his coat. "Now, I have to get back to work. So, deal? Dates traded for man tips and pie?"

She nodded once sharply. "One caveat. I have to know you won't have me wish for anything bad. Like hurting someone or something."

"I promise you I would never." And he wasn't a man who wished to begin with. Wishing was for fools. His sweet tooth, however? That was real.

"You said I should be surprised by what people would 'never' do."

"Touché." She was smart, which made it doubly odd she was after a guy like Russell. The man did not deserve this girl.

He held out his hand. "So, you in?"

She shook it. "I'm in."

"Oh, and one more thing. Let everyone think we're together, including Suzette Marie."

"But—"

"No, Chloe." He knew she'd spill the truth a little too easily, ruining the plan. "You women and your oversharing. It will not help if Suzette Marie tries to help you by backing off anymore. It will only make him want her more. If anything, brag about me." He shrugged on his jacket.

"Ha! Like I ever would..."

"Oh, you will. Whenever she asks. Then, she might let it drop to her fellow workers, like—"

"Russell." Now she beamed. "And he'll get jealous and swoop in? He didn't do that when you kissed me at the basketball game."

"*You* kissed *me*."

"Technicality."

"Which wins cases. He didn't swoop in because we haven't dangled a big enough carrot."

"And you've got the carrot to compete?" She dropped her chin and peered up at him from under her lashes.

Hilarious, Pie Queen. "I got whatever it takes."

She opened her mouth to speak, but he held up his hand, having no time for an answer—and even less interest in arguing with her anymore. "Friday. Get ready to take notes."

"Until then…" She grasped the empty pie tin and pulled it toward her. "Now that you've finished the pie, have a wish to make?"

He did. He wished this girl would open her eyes. But someone else needed it more—even if this wishing thing was bullshit. "I wish for Jorge Fernandez to win the settlement due him."

"Who?"

"He's a client. That's all I can say."

"Okay then." She pushed her arm into the sleeve of her cardigan, the first item of clothing he'd burn. "Get ready to win."

"Get ready to make Russell beg at your feet."

11

"You really should have warned me about the dress code." Her top with the pink and cream flower pattern screamed like a neon sign in the room of blue and black suits and beige sheath dresses. Not to mention she'd brought a homemade chocolate crème pie to this snooty gathering.

His forehead wrinkled. "There is no dress code."

"Oh, yeah?" She slipped her hand free. "All these business suits? And women in mourning clothes?" It was ridiculous, really. She in her pastels and them as polished as makeup counter girls in their black heels and their hair curled up into crisp French twists.

It shocked her no one checked her head for hayseed.

He chuckled. "Never been inside a law firm before?"

"Yes. No." She gave off an exasperated sigh. "You said it was a party."

"I said a wine and cheese. Standing out isn't bad." He grasped her hand and brought it to his lips. He glanced over their joined hands at someone across the room. "Besides, these women wish they could bake as well as you."

She withdrew her hand because *ewww* on the slobbery

PDA. "A party in a conference room?" So little imagination. And anyone could have picked up the little cubes of cheese and carrot sticks at any grocery store. Her pie was the only sugar in the room, and these people could use it. Nerves crackled in the air.

A few women, three to be exact, all had eyes on Nick like they'd like to smear him with chocolate and lick it off. Of course, he stood there with her like a big pink flower, holding her hand, signaling he was on a date, and at least they seemed to get a clue—unlike a certain French teacher had around Chloe's future husband.

Truthfully, the last few days' clusterfudge wasn't Suzette Marie's fault. She didn't ask Russell to go to Paris with her, but it looked like it was happening anyway. According to Betty Ann who worked for Principal Markinson, he'd put in the request first thing Monday morning. Chloe had made Betty Ann her favorite pie, a Boston crème, for that bit of intelligence.

If anyone was to blame, it was Chloe.

First, she'd unwisely lip-locked Nick in front of Suzette Marie and Russell—and now was unable to clear up the matter with her. Or Russell, for that matter.

Second, she'd struck a deal with the devil himself—and she was supposed to brag about him. Having to fake her interest? That alone deserved a prize at the end.

When Suzette Marie had grilled her on Nick, because of course, she would, Chloe still chose honesty.

Where did they first meet? Easy—Peppermint Sweet.

How long have they known each other? Also easy—seems like an eternity.

Was she in love? Not so easy to answer. "Yes, with Russell," sat on her tongue like sugar that refused to melt. To be safe, Chloe shrugged in answer.

She wished like mad Suzette Marie would run to Russell

It Was All The Pie's Fault

and tell him, but so far, he had acknowledged nothing—other than Suzette Marie's presence. Like when she walked into the employee lounge, he acted like the sun had burst through a hurricane or something.

There had to be a way to stop Russell from going to Paris with her. But the number of wishes she needed to make were piling up. She nearly felt buried by them.

Or perhaps she was suffocating from the game she was playing.

But the old proverb clearly states insanity is doing the same thing over and over again and expecting different results. So, here she was. Doing something wildly, ludicrously different to see if she truly was on the right path with Russell.

"So." A silver-haired older gentleman strode up to them. Nick had been staring at the guy all night. "Who is this?" He smiled kindly down at her.

Nick's arm conveniently found its way around her waist. He pulled her closer, which caused an unladylike grunt to leave her throat.

"This is Chloe Hart."

She held out her hand. "Hi. Nice, uh, party."

"So glad you could join us, Miss Hart. I'm Hank Carter. Nick, it's good to see you away from your desk." He leaned toward her. "We don't often get the pleasure of Nick's company at our events. I was beginning to think he disliked them."

She peered up at him. "Oh? We were at a party last weekend."

Mr. Carter seemed quite interested at her words as his eyes widened. "I'm glad to hear that. I understand you're the baker."

"Yes, and—"

"Chloe's pies are special."

Her face swung to the man who said he didn't believe in her wizardry ways. "Thanks, and if you—"

"Enjoy it, you could get them at Peppermint Sweet," Nick filled in quickly.

Hank eyed Nick. "Excellent coffee there. By the way, heard we got a settlement on the construction case."

"Came in today. Generous."

"Bit of a surprise given how adamant they were about going to trial." Hank sliced his eyes toward Chloe as if she wasn't supposed to know details about something obviously confidential. "Looks like your luck is looking up."

"We worked it pretty hard." A muscle in his jaw twitched a little.

The man nodded. "Nice to meet you, Miss Hart. I hope we see you again. Nick." The guy slapped him on the shoulder.

Nick rolled his neck and sighed.

"You got the settlement, didn't you?" She leaned toward him. "The Jose Fernandez case?" she whispered.

"I'm impressed you remembered his name."

She shrugged. "And you said wishes don't work. Is that why you cut me off?" He sounded so serious.

His whole body stilled. "I worked my ass off on that case. Luck had nothing to do with it."

She swallowed, "Of course, you worked hard." Maybe Nick also had a thing about winning. He took it to heart. "I didn't mean to insinuate…"

"I know." He swiped his hand through his hair. "Come on. Dinner, and time to enact the Russell plan."

Good, because the room's funereal energy was coma-inducing. No wonder Nick wanted her as a date—and needed her pie. Winnie the Pooh's Eeyore would have been the life of this meeting-in-disguise party.

12

The small, dark French restaurant with its starched white tablecloths and small alcoves draped in heavy curtains was straight out of a movie set. She and Nick sat in a corner booth as if they were on some super-romantic date. They were *not*. They were on a mission. Tonight was merely the start of her win-Russell-back plan.

He liked her. She was sure of it. She'd just messed it up thanks to the help of the guy now sitting across from her.

During dinner, she'd let Nick do most of the talking—going on and on about his work as if he needed her to understand he was a workaholic. She could tell two steps into that office gathering masquerading as a party he needed to be seen as serious.

"It sounds like that construction firm is horrible," she said between bites of her roasted chicken. "I mean, the guy falls off a girder and they debated about whether to call an ambulance? Who *does* that?"

"Someone who wanted him to go home so they could contest the worker's comp. Or try anyway."

She shook her head. "I didn't think that was possible."

"Anything is possible even if the law is clear."

So, Nick has some redeemable qualities. "Good for you. For helping that man."

"Takes the sting out of the more frivolous cases I'm forced to deal with."

"Sounds like you don't enjoy your work much."

"I do. Winning, as you say men are so interested in, is the point—and wise. The more I win, the more I'll get extra opportunities… elsewhere. Now, about the next two weeks. Getting Russell back."

He sure jumped conversations quickly. She set her fork down. "Two weeks. It'll take that long?"

He leaned back in the booth, sighed, and pushed his empty plate away. "Less if you do everything I tell you to. He'll beg for you."

"What do I do?"

He took a long swallow of red wine, the glass nearly disappearing into his huge hand. Besides working, the man's other sport had to be eating. He inhaled food and drink.

He waited a long second before speaking again, eyeing her with the intensity of a lion sizing up prey.

"Well?" She couldn't wait anymore for his "wisdom" about how she could get Russell back, or rather, *beg at her feet*. Plus, his assessment of her was lingering a little too long in places it shouldn't be lingering at all.

She ducked her head a little so his gaze would move from her boobs to his face.

His eyes finally snapped up. "It's simple. When it comes to women, men care about three things: sex, looking impressive to other males, and leaving their genes behind."

Oh, for the love of… "That's ridiculous."

"No, it makes perfect evolutionary sense. Simple mechanics really. To keep the species going. Nothing more."

She could never, ever be with this guy. They were as

It Was All The Pie's Fault

opposite as the polar ice caps. He was beyond cynical. More like living granite on the inside. But she could put up with two weeks of him. She *could*.

She took in a long breath. "So, that means what exactly? I need to be a walking aphrodisiac?"

He sniffed and cleared his throat. "Sort of. Now, you've got the raw material. We just need to shape it. What are you doing tomorrow?"

"Baking." She was bringing Russell another pie even if Nick didn't believe in its power. "And I'm doing some work for our fall kid's show. All the grades are involved, and Russell and I are on the show committee. During our first meeting on Monday, I'm going to dazzle him with my creativity and how good I am with kids."

"You mean you're going to bring him another pie, aren't you?"

She crossed her arms and refused to answer.

"No pie, Chloe. You're going to dazzle him with something else. We're starting with sex."

A giggle formed in her throat. "Of course, we are."

He leaned forward. "Don't like sex?"

"I love it." *Take that, Nick Hollister.* She still flushed red, and her nervous laughter sat at the back of her throat. She really did laugh at all the wrong times.

He, however, did not laugh. He eyed her like he was thinking about something. Something wicked and dangerous and... A smile played on his lips.

She straightened and forced her wholly inappropriate humor to stay down. "I know where this is going. I am not wearing *eff me* pumps to work." So clichéd. Not to mention she'd kill herself.

He snorted. "*Eff me?*"

"I don't swear." One might leak out around her kids. Once the little mimics learned it was a "bad" word, they'd run up and down the hallway shouting it as if given some universal secret.

"No 'effing,' Chloe. You're going to make him grovel for that. But first, we have to get you ready to go into battle on Monday. I'm coming over tomorrow and we're picking out outfits. No stilettos required."

"What is it with men and the battle metaphors?"

"It's appropriate. And after I get through with you? He's going to fall on his sword."

She sat up. "Do you talk to your clients like this? Get them ready for battle?" His confidence rolled off him in waves. He must make mincemeat out of his opposing sides.

"Only if necessary. Now, two. Looking like he's winning in front of other guys. This is where you're not going to let him win—ever."

She smiled at him. "Along with no effing, right?"

"Right. What you're going to do is let *me* win you—in front of him."

She sucked in a sharp breath and pushed backward. She knew where this was going.

"Relax, Pie Queen. Winning *publicly and proverbially*. In fact, let's start right now."

His gaze sliced toward the door. Her head swiveled just in time to catch Russell and Suzette Marie entering.

Her whole body stiffened. "Why is she here? She said…"

"You bragged about me, didn't you?" His head was nodding slowly up and down. "Good girl. That means Suzette Marie felt she could say 'yes' to Russell."

"No. I most certainly did not *brag*." She glared at Russell's hand on the small of Suzette Marie's back. Chloe was going to throw up.

"Stop staring at them. Talk to me." He clasped her hand across the table.

How had he gotten a hold of her hand? Hold? How about

It Was All The Pie's Fault

full capture? She blinked. "Did you know they'd be here? Together?"

"I asked Russell where he would take a date to impress her. He mentioned he was bringing her here to talk about Paris. Boasted about it. So predictable."

She yanked her hand away. "He hates French food."

"Apparently, she loves this place."

With that figure? She didn't love food enough. If she got close enough, one might get poked in the eye with a rib.

Still… Chloe folded her arms. *Shirty Shingles*. They had a *common goal* already—Paris. She and Russell never got to where they had a together goal. Theirs wouldn't have been visiting France but starting a family and teaching and who knew what else. They'd go to Peppermint Sweet for coffee and croissants—and her pie—and talk about their shared ideas for their dream house.

"Don't mope," Nick said.

"I don't mope."

As soon as Russell slid in beside Suzette Marie on her side of the booth, Nick reached over and grabbed her hand. "That sad face you're giving them will not make Russell jealous. Look like you're having the time of your life. That *I'm* the most fascinating guy in the place."

She faced him and forced her cheeks up in a fake smile. "Oh, yes, Mr. Hollister." Her eyelashes fluttered. "I must make doe eyes with you. You're so handsome. So cavemanly."

Her head wouldn't stay in Nick's direction, however. Her gaze was pulled back to… Oh, my God, Russell had brought one of Suzette Marie's hands to his mouth. He nibbled on her finger. *Ewww…* Chloe yanked her own hand free.

In her periphery, Nick twiddled with the stem of his wine glass. "*Stop* looking at them."

"He's practically eating her fingers." Her forehead tightened. "Aren't we going to go say hello or something?"

He sighed heavily, eased himself out of the booth, and held out his hand to her.

"Oh, good. So, what should I say to them?" She eased herself out. She had half a mind to say something snarky to Russell. Nick *couldn't* be right about him. He'd gotten the wrong signals from her, that was all. But she wished he'd put up more of a fight.

"Nothing. We're dancing."

She sank back down. "There's no dance floor!"

"There is always a dance floor." He pulled her to standing.

13

Chloe's hand nearly disappeared in his as he lifted her arm high and swayed. "Follow my lead."

"People are staring." At least, the elderly couple in the corner were. Russell dined on Suzette Marie's digits and didn't even appear to have noticed. Nick knew better. The man noticed. He loved the spotlight, and for a split second, Nick had it.

"That's the point." He squeezed Chloe's hand until she glanced back up at him.

"You sure you're not doing this for your own ego?"

"Of course, I am. I don't mind sticking it to Russell."

That adorable notch between her eyebrows formed. "You don't like him very much, do you?"

Sharp, this one. "You're right. I don't like him."

He hated the duplicity of Russell or any man who said one thing but didn't mean it. Like workman's comp but not giving it. Like having kids but not taking care of them. Or, like Russell, making women feel like they're the center of the universe and they're not. He'd prove to both Suzette Marie and Chloe they deserved better.

She sighed hot breath onto his shoulder. "How do you know all this will work? And don't tell me it's because you know guys."

"I know people. Like I said, one hour on a basketball court is all I need to know about a man. Every Saturday, he talks about the women he has lined up for the weekend like firewood for his weekend bonfire. And by the look on your face, that's news to you."

"If you know so much..." she sucked in a breath from him twirling her between two tables, "why are *you* single?"

She was direct—and angry. *Good.* He twirled her again and her head swiveled in Russell's direction.

"Stop staring." Jesus, this woman.

She sliced her eyes up to him. "You didn't answer my question."

"I'm single by choice. I'm busy. Working. Trying to make partner, get promoted, and move to the West Coast. Until that happens, I don't want to give anyone short shrift."

"But your work wants to see you settled, don't they?"

He chuffed. "They do."

"It's so you don't leave. Once you have a family, then you're more likely to stick around. Statistics show."

Man, she'd nailed it. His future partners needed to see he was stable, regular, wanting to settle down for good. Somehow, even in this modern age, his firm equated partnership worthiness with him dying to march toward an altar. Showing up with a woman who believed in magic pies, however? He'd keep that little tidbit under wraps.

She licked her lip. "That means they think you're valuable. You must be an excellent attorney." She eased up on tiptoes and smiled up at him. "I'll bet everyone wants you on their cases."

"They do."

It Was All The Pie's Fault

Her bottom pink lip glistened a little in the low light, and her eyes glowed a nice golden-green brown.

Even if he was hellbent on staying single, Chloe intrigued him. He was man enough to admit it. He couldn't stop thinking of the way her pink lips turned down and that little dent between her eyes when he'd suggested she kiss him again in an elementary school hallway, of all places. She positively deserved better than player Russell.

She eased back into his hand that rested on her lower back and peered up at him through her lashes. "I'll bet you win a lot."

"Enough." He hadn't lately, but the recent case disappointments were merely a minor setback. He spun her, and her long hair fanned out behind her. She finally got it out of that bun.

She was pretty. He had that right. But she didn't show off her assets, like her spectacular curves that sloped and fell and rose again—precisely the way he liked his women. His hand tightened on hers, more from keeping himself from sliding his fingers where they shouldn't go than anything else.

"How does it feel to have so many futures in your hands, Mr. Hollister?"

His hands felt great right now. In fact, he was going to need a release after this night.

"Pretty good, actually." Truth be told, he enjoyed his work, enjoyed helping people.

"I'm sure you're amazing at it." She batted her eyelashes and then sobered. "How was that? Flirty enough?"

Shit. He was being played. "It'll do. Now, look at me and think about when you knew Russell was your soul mate."

She sighed heavily, let her eyes soften, and her lips relaxed into a slight smile.

"That's better." He chuckled a little. "You women and your 'soul mates.'"

Her look of pure adoration vanished. "You know, if it weren't for women, I doubt men could keep the planet going."

"You're right there." He had no doubts on that front. Look at all his mother had done for him—until his stepfather ended her life too young. That fact drove him straight to the law school path.

He spun Chloe, and his hand found that spot right above her waist where it dipped and then fanned out to her pert ass. She'd look spectacular in a pencil skirt, one that curved over her behind, and when she walked, the bottom would fan left to right.

His hand shifted a little, wanting to feel that divot at the base of her spine. She was, what, a size twelve? He let his fingers span across her back.

She'd also look great in a softer pastel than the bright pink, more like a pale yellow dress that hugged her form, something with a deep V down the front. Sarah at L'Orangerie would know the thing if they stopped by tomorrow and picked up something for her.

Chloe stilled. "What are you doing?"

He pulled her closer, "Nothing."

She gasped and pulled her head back. "You were copping a feel."

A laugh bubbled up. Jesus, little got by this girl. Russell most definitely wouldn't know what to do with this woman.

"I'm appreciating."

"*Appreciating* is not part of our deal."

Oh, yeah, her school librarian voice was getting him hard. "You said no kissing. You didn't say—"

"Don't finish that sentence."

Truth, he shouldn't go there, even in his mind. He barely had time for what little help he'd give her, let alone a relationship. In fact, he should be at the office right now. "Let's go, Chloe. And don't look at them."

After laying a few bills on the table, he grasped her hand to get her attention. She couldn't help herself, could she? She kept sneaking looks over at Russell and Suzette Marie.

They'd noticed Nick and Chloe were here, as well. And Russell had most definitely caught the way his hand roamed Chloe's back. She'd scored tonight and didn't even know it.

Nick drove her back to his law offices and made sure she got into her car. Before she sped away, he settled his forearms on her window edge.

"Give me your phone."

She sighed and handed it over—reluctantly. "If you change my ringtone…"

He chuckled and tapped in his number. "Text me your address and a good time to swing by tomorrow. I get up early, for the record."

"I'm usually up by six every day of the week, so I do the same on the weekends. Makes Mondays less heinous. And I get a head start on baking."

He handed her phone back to her. "I'll bring the coffee, say, around 7:30 if you bake something for us. Then, we start." He straightened.

"You didn't tell me about number three. Leaving your genes behind."

"That one will get resolved if you fix numbers one and two. So, get ready to win him back."

She shook her head. "I can't believe you believe in all this."

"I can't believe you believe in magic pies, as good as they are."

"Your loss. But tell you what. I'll give your manly tenets a try if you give my wishing a try."

He couldn't help but chuckle. "You'll see how well they work. Like you said, get ready to win."

"Then I better make extra pies this weekend." She raised her window, her smile beaming at him from behind the glass.

She really was adorable. Lost as shit, but adorable. After he got through with her tomorrow? She'd be on her way to winning the game. Maybe then she'd wise up about Russell the tomcat.

14

Chloe opened the oven. The juices from the sausage sizzled and the heavenly smell of her favorite breakfast pie rose with the steam. Too bad Russell and Suzette Marie couldn't get a bite of this one, though she was pretty sure sausage was on the woman's *non-non* list. Last night, her fingers, however, seemed very much on the menu.

Chloe had been up since five a.m., unable to sleep, thinking about all Nick had said about men and specifically, Russell. Maybe she didn't know him at all, like how he nibbled women's fingers in public. She was sure Russell was not a PDA guy—at least not *her* Russell. Maybe the bewitched one… Still, something niggled at her about him. Like how he could seem so into Chloe and then suddenly have his head turned so easily.

She reminded herself she'd started this quest to see what could happen with him. She'd see it through. She had to at least try. Otherwise, she'd always wonder if they could have worked it all out if only she'd stuck with him a bit longer. Nana had always said to give people a second chance.

She set the pie on the stovetop—quickly—as heat seeped

through her oven mitt. "Ow." She yanked her hand from Nana's old mitt and sucked on a finger. It would have been smart to get a new one years ago, but she couldn't let go of the tattered black mitt with the faded cherry print.

As she ran water, she began her magic pie mantra, but the soft chime of her doorbell interrupted. 7:30 a.m. on the dot.

"At least you're on time," she said to no one as she made her way to the front door.

She opened it. Nick thrust two large paper cups displaying "Peppermint Sweet" on the side her way.

After waving him inside, she took one drink from his outstretched arm. "I hope you eat sausage."

"Ah, breakfast of champions." He winked. "Smells amazing. Your entire building must be drooling." His gaze roamed over her tiny apartment. "Your place looks like you."

"I suppose you have one of those condos in an all-glass building downtown."

"It's not all glass."

"I'm sure it's perfectly modern and industrial and partner-worthy."

He picked up a pillow gifted to her by her students last year that read *It takes a big heart to teach little minds*. "Huh." He set it down next to Nana's quilt folded at the end of her simple loveseat.

"Okay, put away that disapproving face if you want any breakfast. Hungry?" she asked.

"Relax. I'm not judging. And I'm always hungry." He settled his huge frame down on the barstool in front of her kitchen banquet—the only real dining space she had. "So, no hocus pocus wishing pie this morning?" He pointed at the pan that still had steam rising from it.

His cynicism wouldn't undo her. "It's a savory, and the wishing works with all of Nana's recipes, so get yours ready, esquire." She lifted her spatula. "Big piece or gigantic piece?"

It Was All The Pie's Fault

He arched an eyebrow. "You need to ask? And right now, I wish for the coffee to kick in."

"You work a lot, don't you?" She cut him an enormous piece.

"So do you. Teaching and baking?"

"Oh, I don't view what I do as work. It's fun."

He chuckled a little. "You're unique, Chloe. I'll give you that."

"Ooo, such a flatterer, Nicholas Adam Hollister." She set down a plate that barely held all the sausage pie.

"You looked me up online." He wasted no time putting a huge forkful of the pie in his mouth and then murmured it was good.

"Of course, I did."

He swallowed. "Good girl. Always Google the men you let in your house." He took another huge bite.

"Yeah, well, you're the first guy here in a while."

"I thought your former boyfriend Russell would have been here at least." He waved a fork at her kitchen cabinet. "Ya know, he should have taken care of that. Nice dishes."

The door didn't latch and bared her mismatched china found at various flea markets to the world. She was shocked he noticed.

"Russell has never been here." She took a small bite of pie. One should never rush eating sausage. "We just had our first date, remember? At Peppermint Sweet where we also first met."

He set his fork down, leaned back, and picked up his coffee cup. "Chloe. Man lessons starting right now. Never, *ever* meet a guy you already know, who you work with, who asks you out, *somewhere*. He picks you up. At the door. And if on the first date he doesn't open the car door for you, it's over before it started."

"Wow, so old-fashioned."

"Basic manners."

She snorted. "Maybe for 1950. I can tell you've been single a while. No guy does that stuff anymore."

"Oh, they do. When they're really into someone."

Come to think of it, Russell was always opening the door for Suzette Marie, probably more to make sure she didn't whap herself in the eye with it. Yeah, her sense of sisterhood with the woman was waning.

"Okay. Fine. I'll let him open the door." It would be nice, actually, to have someone do something for her.

"And make this sausage pie. It's amazing." He grinned at her and took another huge forkful. Nick wasn't like she thought. He had his moments. He would be caustic one second and charming the next. "But next time, make it larger."

The guy also had a bottomless stomach.

She closed her eyes and silently recited the mantra. She had to play fair, right? And Nick's wishes were as valid as anyone else's.

To all who eat
    This salt and sweet
    I bless your wish
    With my dish.
    If good and true
    It comes to you.
    Embrace the light
    And take a bite.

"What was that?"

She snapped her eyes open to find Nick staring at her.

"Sending your wish out into the world."

It Was All The Pie's Fault

He harrumphed. "So, these pies are all your grandmother's recipes?" He scraped up the last bit on his plate.

She nodded. "Yep. And don't be so cynical. Nana's magic is powerful."

"You still bake with her?"

Her fist found its way to her sternum. "She died three years ago." She'd thought the hole that Nana's death left had closed somewhat over the last few years. It hadn't.

He stilled. "I'm sorry. You miss her."

"Every day." More than she thought possible. "She'd lived a good life. It was purposeful, bringing food every Saturday to people who couldn't leave their houses, especially pies. 'They all need some homemade goods. To know people care,' she said. You have family here in town, Nick?"

"Nope. Just one sister and her son. They live in Trent County, about a hundred miles away. I'm trying to get her to move closer."

"Sorry. What about her husband? You get along?"

He wiped his mouth with a napkin. "Not since I slapped a restraining order on him."

"Oh." She didn't know what to say. Should she ask him more about it? He didn't look like he wanted to elaborate.

Nick reached for a huge piece of pie. Chloe turned to the stove to heat up water for tea. She should put on a pot of coffee for Nick as the dark circles under his eyes didn't seem one bit affected by Peppermint Sweet's fabulous shade-grown coffee. The man worked too much, but then, who was she to judge in that department?

He finally shoved his plate away. "Chloe, I'm serious about you switching careers here."

"No way. I love my kids." She faced him.

"It shows." He eyed her and ran his finger over his lips.

She crossed her arms. "Is this the part where you tell me I look like I stepped out of Little House on the Prairie?"

"No, more like you're hiding." He stood and arched his back in a stretch. "Okay, Baking Goddess, to your closet. We're moving into phase two. You're going to show me your goods..."

She laughed. "My *goods* are off-limits."

A huge grin spread across his face and he rounded the small island. "Come on, Chloe Hart. Let's liberate the hot librarian." He placed his hands on her shoulders and steered her to the hallway leading to her bedroom. "You've got a closet full of whips back there. I can feel it."

Man, was he going to be disappointed. "Those are off-limits to you, too."

At least that earned a laugh from him, which was insulting but accurate. Silver chains and black leather were not her colors.

15

Nick threw himself across her bed, instantly making her queen-size bed appear child-size. "Okay, show me what you got."

She knew where this closet visit was headed. "First, you have to take an oath to not laugh. No acting like Simon Cowell on a bad day."

"Oh, I'm going to be judging. You're going to give me a fashion show so we can see what we're keeping and what we're tossing." He toed off his expensive shoes and plopped himself on her bed again. This man dropped his clothes with ease, didn't he?

He really was a large man—and he was *on her bed*. She pulled her top from her clammy chest. It was hot in here.

"Chloe. Trust me." He then propped his head on his hand and pulled her penguin plush pillow to his chest.

It was hard to trust a guy who hugged a plushie. "For the record, not wearing an eff me outfit."

His face broke into a huge grin. "Oh, yes, you are. To Friday's wine and cheese where I'll make all my colleagues jealous with your bodalicious body."

She snorted. "Sure. So bodalicious."

"Sweetheart, you have a body that men only dream about."

"Liar." But she liked that his charming side was back. "No touching. No smutty times, remember?"

"No physical sex."

"Is there any other kind?"

His characteristic smirk was back. "Oh, yes. In my mind."

"Stop it. Stop it right now." She shook her finger at him and his eyes fired—playfully. *There was going to be no playing here, Mister.* "I belong to Russell and you cannot..." she spluttered.

"Relax. I'm only messing with you. Look..." He eased down to the end of the bed and sat upright before her. "You got the hot saint thing down. Now, you got to throw in some seasoning like... whatever you put in your pies... cinnamon and stuff..." He waved his hand.

She grasped his fingers. Oh, strong. Even his hands were solid. "Cinnamon and... stuff?" She swallowed and let go of him.

"Yeah, the sinner angle. What are the equivalents of sinner ingredients?" He eased back onto his elbows looking far, far too comfortable lazing on a comforter dotted with daisies.

"No such thing. It's all good."

He snapped his fingers. "There, you made my point. Bring out both sides of yourself because both are good. Now, since you'll mostly be seeing Russell at work, show me your fanciest work clothes."

She dropped her chin and peered over her nose at him. Fanciest? Did he not see her six-year-old students? He could not expect a Badgley Mischka cocktail dress to leap off her hangers. "These." She turned to her closet and pulled out the blouse and black skirt she'd worn at Peppermint Sweet.

It Was All The Pie's Fault

"Oh, yes, the first date black skirt." He rolled his eyes.

"I almost wore these." She brought out her nicest khakis.

"Tell me you would not wear khakis on a date." The man actually groaned. "Those pants are for people who work behind rental car counters. I don't ever want to see another beige thing on you."

Had he never looked around his office? "Tell that to your firm's admirers."

"What admirers?"

"All those women in their fade-into-the-wallpaper sheath dresses eyeing you like a menu item." She batted her eyelashes. "I saw them sizing me up. I swear that if the super-tall one with the pinchy nose thought she could take me, she would probably jump me in the ladies' room."

"An attorney wouldn't risk it." He scoffed. "And they are colleagues. Nothing more." He launched himself to standing and in two steps stood before her small closet. "I see you have the requisite hundred black pants. *Women*. I swear." He shook his head and began to swipe hangers across the metal rod.

"What's wrong with black pants?"

"Nothing if they're tight enough, but that's not why women wear them. You wear them to look skinny. If you ladies only realized how much we loved your butts."

The fact that he said "butt" made her giggle for some odd reason. What was it with her laughing around this guy?

He turned to her. "Where is that cherry print skirt?"

"You liked it?" That would be a surprise.

"Loved it."

Sadness spread through her limbs like a stain. "So does Russell. Or so I thought."

He reached into her closet and swiped some hangers. "Now this..." He pulled out a skirt she'd forgotten she had. It was a dark gray straight skirt with a row of buttons up the side. His large fingers rubbed the materials. "Good quality."

She hung it back up. "And completely inappropriate for teaching first graders. I can barely bend over in this thing." In fact, why did she have it at all?

He pulled it back out. "What time is this committee meeting of yours?"

"Three-thirty p.m., right after the kids get loaded on the busses. Why?"

He held up the skirt. "You're changing into this right before your committee meeting. Consider it... your magic skirt. You can say it's for a date later. But don't tell him who with when he asks."

"He won't ask."

"Oh, he will. But you won't say. You'll smile and wink. It will make him wonder. And..." He reached in and grabbed a white cashmere sweater set, one she'd also completely forgotten about because *white*. "Wear this on top."

Was he cray-cray? "I would never wear this to work. It'd be covered in marker by ten a.m." She'd never wink to answer a question, either. "And I don't wink."

"You do now. The idea is to make him *wonder*."

She sighed but moved to the bathroom to put on the inappropriate garments. Once he saw them on her, he'd realize how she resembled that sausage he ate this morning.

Still, she squeezed herself into it and shuffled back to her bedroom. She placed her hands on her hips. "It's a little tight, don't you think?"

"Yep, that's going to do the magic."

"Thought you didn't believe in it."

"In that outfit, I'd believe anything. Now, what else you got?"

She had to say this about Nick. He was definitive albeit

It Was All The Pie's Fault

picky. As she tried on outfit after outfit, he finally found four he liked for her "week's wardrobe" as he labeled it.

He picked normal but form-fitting items. She'd have never thought to pair her blue sheath dress with her jeans jacket that he deemed "cool chick." The gray shirt and wholly impractical white sweater, black dress pants with a top that had a similar flounce around the neckline of Suzette Marie's ruined one, and a purple wrap dress she'd forgotten she owned also made the cut.

She was going to need to bring a suitcase to work every day.

∽

"Okay." He glanced at his watch. Shit, he needed to get to work. "Show me this last one. This one is for Friday night. Then I got to go."

She rounded the corner, and his spine straightened. He stood.

She smoothed down the front of the cocktail dress. "I know. It's not sexy enough—"

"You're wearing that one." He walked around her. "But only on Friday with me."

The white lace overlaid a similar background that gave the illusion of wearing nothing but lace but not showing much. The V-neckline wasn't too revealing, and the A-line skirt skimmed her hips at the perfect angle.

He slowly nodded his head. "We have to ratchet up poor Russell slowly. Come out of the gates with this and he'll have a heart attack."

She smiled up at him, and their eyes locked—for a long second.

Finally, she cleared her throat. "Time to get out of this, I guess." She paused in the doorway. "On Friday, are we going back to that French place? So he'll be guaranteed to see?"

An odd feeling arose. Russell would run his gaze up and down her body in that dress. Old Russell was getting a gift, really. Getting to view Chloe in all her glory.

"No." Nick would make sure the guy got an eyeful of Chloe as she walked away—and toward him because an idea dawned. "Chloe, either I or my car service will pick you up after your meeting tomorrow."

"You can do that?" Her eyes lit up. "Wait." Her eyes narrowed. "You're not pulling up to Broadstreet Elementary in a dick-ousine, are you? I don't want to draw attention that way."

He chortled. "A dick-ousine?"

"The size of the limo is in direct proportion with the guys…" she waved at his crotch, "thing, only in reverse."

This woman was funny without trying. He leaned closer. "Then I'd have to send you a Mini Cooper."

She flushed anew and her eyes widened. And damned if his ego didn't fill up to full strength at her response.

"No limos. More like a glorified Uber. Does that work for you?"

"Your boss won't get mad?"

"My boss will love the fact I'm using company assets for a woman. He is all about them—especially the stable kind."

"You know, you're the only man I know who can make an insult sound like a compliment. Or was that a compliment turned to an insult?" She tapped her chin. "Either way, keep your marriage thoughts to yourself. I'm taken."

"Not yet, Pie Queen." And maybe never given what he knew about Russell. "Expect a car coming for you after your work ends every day. And when good old Russ sees me dropping you off every morning, he'll think—"

It Was All The Pie's Fault

She gasped.

Russell would think they slept together. Yes, it was mind fuckery, and he fucking loved it. "That's the point, Chloe girl."

He sat, pulled his shoes back on quickly, and stood again. "Time to go."

She shifted on her feet. "Joining the guys for basketball?"

"Skipping it. Let Russell wonder where I am. If I'm here with you." And this had been way more fun than pounding a ball and glowering at Russell.

Her throat moved in a swallow. "You are here with me."

That he was. They stared at one another for a long second. She had a smattering of freckles across her nose. If only women understood covering up such little unique touches wasn't necessary.

She spun suddenly, a red flush growing across her chest.

She walked him to the door, her bare feet with her bubblegum pink toenails making soft slapping noises on the hardwood floor. The lace dress swished with her movements, a seductive rustle he'd always loved. Of course, the *zlip* of a zipper being lowered was better.

She cracked open her front door to let him out. "How do you know about clothes, anyway? I mean, most men don't."

"I bought most of my sister's clothes in high school."

"You did?"

Why did he tell her that? Those weren't his favorite years to reminisce about. "Now, about your committee meeting. You're going to be late for it." He pointed a finger at her. "So you can make an entrance in that bodalicious gray skirt."

One side of her mouth lifted. "Is that an official term? Bodalicious?"

"If it's not, it should be."

She leaned her cheek against the door's edge. "Hey, you

didn't tell me what your wish is for the sausage breakfast today."

"I wish…" He paused and stared at her. "I wish for you to turn Russell's head."

Not really, but it's what she wanted.

16

"Thanks, Susan." He returned his phone to its cradle. Now that he had secured a regular car for Chloe for the entire week, he could get to work.

Law firms would do anything to keep a guy working. Car service, meal service; hell, he wouldn't be surprised if they'd set up a bed in his office if he asked for one. That last one was ironic given how much his partners seemed like marriage—and staying out of the office most weekends—was the end-all-be-all of life these days.

He returned his attention to his yellow legal pad. If he didn't get this brief done today, tomorrow would pile up on him like a mudslide. And he needed to be productive so he could attend that wine and cheese on Friday with Chloe on his arm in her hot dress.

That fucking dress. The way the lace flounced on the back and the fabric slid over her butt... Smoking. But his favorite garment of hers was still her cherry print skirt topped with her white sweater. He loved it.

He slammed the portfolio shut. He wasn't helping her in order to *love* anything.

Maybe he'd take a walk around the block, move that sausage pie around, get his head cleared of Chloe in pencil skirts and tight jeans.

He stood and grabbed his jacket. His cell phone rang, a familiar number filling the screen.

"Hey, sis, something wrong?" If her dirtbag ex dared to violate the restraining order, he'd add yet another task to his Saturday to-do list.

"Can't I call my brother without something being wrong?"

"Of course." His ears strained to hear any male voices in the background. She'd had to call him and pretend everything was fine before when it clearly wasn't. "No sign of—"

"Nope. Like I said, he got the message. We're fine. You're at work again, aren't you?"

"Was about to head out." To get a certain woman out of his head.

"Good." She sighed heavily into the phone. "Just make sure you have a life."

"I am." He leaned back in his chair. "In fact, you'll be happy to know I met a girl."

She let off a squeal. "Oh, that's great. What's her name? What's she do?"

Maybe he shouldn't have said anything. He was usually better at anticipating a line of questioning. He normally didn't talk about women with his sister. "Chloe. She teaches first grade… and bakes." He almost said *magic pies* but didn't. He rather enjoyed keeping that secret. Not that she ever balked at telling people her beliefs.

Daphne laughed. "You do surprise me, Nick." A small child's voice sounded in the background. "Benjamin, baby, I'll be right there…"

"Hey, tell the little man I'm going to come see you… soon." When, he'd never know. It'd be so much easier if she'd at least move closer. He'd told her repeatedly he'd pay for it.

"You might be able to tell him yourself. I've been considering your offer. You may be right. About moving?"

His hand that'd been twiddling with a pen stilled. "Tell me you will and I'll make it happen. You could move here first. I've got the space and then we could all go out west in a few months."

She laughed softly. "Whoa there. Just considering. I'm not sure about L.A. But Moorsville?"

"Do it, Daph. It's… nice here." A sentence he'd never believed he'd utter, but it wasn't a lie. Damn, Chloe must be getting to him.

"Ever the protective older brother. I'd have to find a job…"

"Let me handle all that." He'd shuffle through his old client list. Surely, someone could hire Daphne. Of course, he didn't know her capabilities except for throwing parties for her deadbeat ex. "What would you like to do?"

"Do? For the last three years all I've done is cook, clean, and arrange flowers for…" She didn't say her ex-husband's name. That was good, or that ever-present knot in his stomach at the image of the bruises on Daphne's face might snap his good mood today in two.

"I've got you covered, Daph. Don't I always?"

"You do. Make sure you're covering yourself, too, okay? Have fun with your new girl."

Covering himself? Come to think of it, that's all he ever did. "About that job… Let me ask around. I'll get back to you in a day or two."

"Thanks, Nick."

After he killed the call, he rose. His new girl, huh? Chloe wasn't his. But for someone "not his," he sure couldn't shake the image of her in that dress.

He began to pace. He needed that walk. *Now.* Maybe he'd swing by Peppermint Sweet and see if they needed some help that Daphne could provide. While he was there, maybe he'd buy some pie.

17

Chloe jumped up once more to get the skirt over her hips and banged her elbow against the metal bathroom stall. "Gah, ow."

She sucked in a breath and let it out to see if she could breathe in the skirt. It fit like it had over the weekend—barely. In her house, it felt okay, but here? About to go public? She peered over her shoulder at her behind. Nick Hollister was ridiculous. A sausage casing was sexier.

She tapped out a message on her phone.

<<I can't do it.>>

Three dots appeared and then disappeared. *Yeah, Mr. I Know Men* couldn't be bothered. But then, a message popped up.

<<Put it on, Pie Queen.>>

She gasped and glanced around as if there might be cameras.

<< I look like a sausage.>>

<<Bodalicious, remember?>>

Gooey warmth filled her inside.

<<If this doesn't work, no more pie for you.>>

<<Why would I risk such a thing by lying to you?>>

Sugar beets. She was going to have to go out and do it. Before she could reply to him, another text came in.

<<Send me a picture.>>

No effing way. Photographic evidence of the bratwurst she resembled?

<<You've already seen it.>>

<<Chicken>>

The fricking nerve of this guy.

<<AM NOT>>

<<Atta girl>>

She walked right into that one. Was it Shakespeare who wrote "kill all the lawyers?"

She peeked her head out of the bathroom stall. She was alone. Maybe she'd see how bad it was in the mirror.

If the look was terrible, she'd put her khaki pants back on. Better to look like a rental car counter girl than the reason girdles were invented. She could always squeeze herself into the gray skirt before Nick's car service showed up. Let him have a gander of the *wurst* outfit.

She stepped out and waddled up to the mirror. She pivoted. Okay, no panty lines. That was good. But really? The fabric scooped over her ass. Too much?

The door cracked open, and Suzette Marie pranced inside. She stopped at seeing Chloe. "Allo, Chloe." She eyed her up and down, her eyes wide and curious. "So dressy. You look great."

"Um, thanks."

She moved closer. "I'm glad to catch you, too. About dinner on Friday... What you saw."

"Oh, don't worry about it. I know... I mean, I *imagine* you needed to talk about Paris, right?" That was it, right?

Suzette Marie let out a long breath, lines around her eyes

It Was All The Pie's Fault

softening. "Yes. That was all. I am not interested in him. He is so…"

"Into you?" Chloe might as well lay it out.

"I was going to say pushy. But we did need to talk so…" She shrugged and placed her hands on Chloe's shoulders. "You have Nick now. So handsome."

He was, but who cared? "Sort of. I'm keeping my options open." There, that would be something Nick would approve of, and it wasn't a lie. Let Suzette Marie give Russell the message her door was still open.

"Good woman." Suzette Marie lowered her beautiful lashes in a slow wink. "And that skirt really does look amazing on you."

Okay, maybe Chloe could wear the hip hugger. "See you later, Suzette Marie." She grasped her bag and headed out.

She'd send a quick text to Nick. For extra courage.

<<I might be late when Russell falls at my feet like you promised he would>>

<<Nix on the late to your dick-ousine. He shows interest? Wink. Walk away.>>

Bull spit. Really? She wouldn't have the willpower. Plus, she did not wink. It wasn't her "look." And swear to God, if he sent a stretch monstrosity to embarrass her, she'd withhold all pies for him forever.

Better yet, she'd conveniently forget to add sugar.

Her phone buzzed again, the nag.

<< Walk. Away.>>

He was a mind reader, somehow knowing her willpower to do such a thing was tenuous as best.

<<Yeah, yeah.>>

She slipped her phone into her bag.

As she neared the gymnasium, the familiar squeak of rubber soles on the floor and pounds of a basketball mixed with adolescent male and female voices. But it was one voice that lured her like a beacon. Russell's voice carried over Bradley's barking cheers to his students who'd stayed for their basketball training.

At the far end of the court, Russell, Blanche Miller, the second grade art teacher, and Tip Howard, the new fourth grade history teacher, huddled on the bleacher stands. Russell wore the shirt that brought out the blue in his eyes—her favorite one of his.

She walked slowly toward them, mostly because the unforgiving fabric demanded tiny steps. She acted like it was to make sure she didn't get whapped by a basketball.

Blanche noticed her first. "Chloe, help me outvote these guys. We can't have my class painting all the sets without some help. Not unless you want to put this show on next year instead. Have you ever seen a seven-year-old with a paintbrush? It's dried before they get to the next swipe."

"My first graders can help. They do everything fast."

"I'm sure their parents will love getting their kids back coated in paint." Russell made room for her on the bleacher. "Hey, Chloe. We were talking about where to slot the kids."

"Oh? Painting?"

"That's what kids do, get covered in paint and dirt." Tip smiled and leaned back, eyeing her. "Someone looks nice today."

"Yes, you do. White is a great color for you," Blanche said.

"So, my class can help you," Russell added

Blanche cleared her throat. "Guys." She lifted a finger and pointed at her head. "Art teacher here. Let's let the kids who *want* to paint paint? Any grade, any child. Those who want to be on stage can."

"Exactly." Chloe nodded toward her. "Now, I have an idea." With some effort, Chloe managed to sit. "Let's have my first graders be the animal menagerie in the back. They really only care about being included and wearing a fun costume. They don't need to say a word."

"We could end up with fairies and unicorns," Russell snorted.

"Even better. It will make the spring theme more interesting. We need to spice it up."

"Rather unconventional. But we need at least one bluebird. It's the school mascot." He eyed her from head to toe. Jesus, did she look like a stuffed bird? Probably.

"Volunteering, Langston?" Tip asked him.

Russell lifted his chin. "Costume would fit you better."

Chloe swiped her hair to the side of her neck and tried not to fidget too much. Now she remembered why she never wore this sweater set. Cashmere itched.

"By the way, Chloe," Tip said. "Your pie was amazing the other day."

Blanche nodded. "It was. Was that mango in there?"

"Why, yes. Special recipe. Did you have some, Russell?" She blinked at him.

"Nah. Sorry. Still training"

Tip slapped his leg. "Man, if only my wife liked to bake."

"I'm sorry you didn't get any, Russell." Chloe cocked her head. "You on a special diet during training?" She just needed a list of ingredients he'd ingest. She could make a pie out of anything.

Tip's forehead wrinkled at that news. "Don't let my wife hear about you being on diet. She'll put me on one before I know it." He patted his considerable belly.

Russell chuffed. "Lay off the beer, perhaps?"

"Yeah, I hear you prefer French wine these days."

Blanche and Chloe rolled their eyes at one another as if saying, *"men."* Blanche leaned over to her and whispered, "Have a date or something?"

Chloe smiled. "Or something."

Russell side-eyed her. So, she winked like Nick said to. He must have planted the suggestion in her brain because winking wasn't her style. Was he now hypnotizing her?

Russell blinked in her direction.

Oh. He noticed... something. Nick had been right. What was the next step? With a mental snap of her fingers, she remembered. *Walk away.*

She rose. "So, my kids will be the menagerie, and let me know if you need help on painting, Blanche. I might be able to. Sorry to run, but I have to go."

"Oh, you *do* have a date," Blanche cooed.

"Maybe. See you all tomorrow." With any luck, she wouldn't hobble on her low heels. Thank God Nick didn't force her to put on anything higher than a one-inch pump. She still hobbled a little. The thought Russell might be watching sent jitters down to her toes.

Once she was through the gymnasium doorway, she blew out a long breath she'd been holding.

"Hey, Chloe." Russell's voice boomed behind her.

Her belly danced. Could Nick have been right? She slowly turned.

Russell swept his beautiful blue eyes down and back up at her. "Interesting idea on letting your kids be the menagerie."

She tamped down the sigh that wanted to rise up over how fabulous that shirt really did look on him.

"But are you sure they should choose their own? I mean, we could end up with a bunch of penguins and polar bears and off-season things." He sniffed.

She'd not seen this judgmental side of Russell before. "Would that be so bad?"

"It's a little... out of control, don't you think?"

"Hmm. Maybe I like out of control." She smiled without showing teeth.

It Was All The Pie's Fault

"You?" He bumped her shoulder with his. "You've likely got the next thirty years mapped out."

And why would he think that? It was true, but the words landed like stones in her belly. "I've got to catch my ride." She then winked at him. Again? The stupid wink just... came out.

Oh, my God, if Nick cursed her somehow, she'd never forgive him. She moved to turn away, though her entire body wanted to stay planted before Russell even if he was in an oddly pedantic mood. Still, she'd promised Nick she'd follow his plan.

"But..." Russell started.

She didn't give in to the pull to stay. She walked away because *score!* He'd followed her into the hallway. Her ego lit up a little at that fact.

In the parking lot, she stepped up to the black sedan idling by the sidewalk.

Nick Hollister himself stepped out.

"Oh, I thought it was going to be your car service."

He glanced at the school. "Insurance in case you lost your willpower to walk away."

She quickly glanced back to see if Russell was there. He wasn't.

"Stop staring." Then he swooped his other arm over his BMW. "Car. At your service." He jogged around to her side. "Miss Hart." He opened the door for her.

She quickly glanced backward again—in case Russell followed her.

Nick placed a finger on her chin and turned her face to him. He waggled a finger.

Yeah, yeah. She was *looking* again. "Thank you." She got in, and with a supreme willpower worthy of the Queen's guard, she didn't glance back at the school again to check to see if Russell appeared.

As Nick eased into the driver's seat, he smiled at her. "So, did he spot anything different?"

"Your wish came true. He noticed me." He was such a cranky-pants today, too.

He peered into his rearview mirror. "*My* wish?"

"After breakfast. You said you wished for him to notice me, and he did."

His head fell back against the headrest. "That was all you, Chloe girl." He spun the steering wheel with his palm. "Now, tomorrow, you're not going to show up at the meeting at all."

"What? I can't do that." She was not about to abandon her duties.

"Then be late again."

She sighed heavily. "That, I can do. How was your day? You look chipper."

He laughed. "It was alright…" A beat of silence hung in the air. "Had some good things happen."

"You winning cases?" She waggled her eyebrows.

"Yes. And before you say it was your 'abracadabra,' the win came from hard work."

"Yep. It couldn't *possibly* be magic." She rolled her eyes at him. "Except my day kind of was. Thank you very much."

He squeezed her hand. "I knew it."

Warmth seeped through her skin as his fingers curled around hers for one long second. It was nice, two comrades in arms fighting counterforces to their desires. To have a partner in romantic crime. Even if their goals were so different, their partnership seemed to be working. It sure had sped things up. Before, her progress with Russell moved like a sloth. In fact, glaciers had moved faster.

He returned his grip to the steering wheel. "So, tell me everything."

She recounted every detail to Nick, who grew silent but appeared to be listening intently.

As they pulled up to her apartment building, she was nearly out of breath. "But then..."

"What?"

"Oh, it's nothing." Russell's agitation was a mere blip. She unbuckled her seat belt. "So, what's next?"

"Keep doing what you're doing. Wear the outfits, especially your confident face. Ignore him. Either I or a car will pick you up every day. By Thursday, I'll know the next steps." He cracked open his door.

He circled around the car, opened her car door for her, and helped her out.

"Thanks. Hey, you have a favorite pie? I owe you one for this week, right?"

He rubbed his finger over his five o'clock shadow. "Pecan."

"Consider it done. Extra magic."

He puffed air through his smile and then circled back to his driver's side. "See you tomorrow, Chloe."

And tonight, she'd bake. She was too high to go to bed early. After she peeled off the pencil skirt, that was. She needed to breathe to roll out pie crust.

18

Chloe stepped out of the taxicab and onto the sidewalk. She peered up at the building with Weeks, Shipman, and Carter's name proudly displayed on its side. "All that glass and cement." The sterile building suited Nick with its sharp lines and smug presentation. It screamed, "Nothing to do here but work."

She glanced down at the pecan pie covered in tin foil and nestled in a red and white-checked hand towel. "Pie, you and I are going to bring a bit of normalcy to Nick Hollister's life." He deserved something nice since he'd helped her enjoy a minor win with Russell yesterday.

But then, Nick didn't pick her up this morning. Of course, he hadn't promised it would be him every day.

Instead, a very nice gentleman named Michael sporting a hipster ponytail pulled up in a black sedan in front of her apartment building, presented a Weeks, Shipman, and Carter card, and whisked her to the school.

So, Mohammed, mountain. Here she was.

Wind whipped her black dress pants around her legs, and the flounce on her top kept lifting and smacking her chin. It

It Was All The Pie's Fault

was a "Nick approved" outfit and as impractical as she thought. At least it was a half-teaching day today.

Her students had "final exams" this morning, which was nothing more than a few quizzes for first graders. This afternoon, she had meetings, including the spring fling event planning committee where she'd get to see Russell—one she was now going to be *super-late* for. Parent-teacher conferences filled her schedule for the evening.

Two gentlemen rushed over to help her push open the big glass door.

"Thank you," she whispered as she entered the enormous foyer.

The click-clack of high heels and the scuffs of expensive leather shoes echoed in the cavernous marble lobby. The ceilings had to be three stories tall, with several open, galley-like walkways so people on the first two floors could look down on the people in the lobby like watching pretty fish go by.

Everyone was so dressy. Women in tight sheath dresses with long ropes of gold necklaces and hair pulled up in chignons. Men in suit coats and shiny shoes. Not a single pair of jeans was in sight.

She pulled her top up a little in a vain attempt to hide more of her cleavage. It was futile. She approached the woman behind the moon-shaped receptionist desk. "Hello, my name is Chloe Hart. I'm here to see Nick Hollister?"

"Is he expecting you?" She didn't return the smile. Probably because it'd hurt. Her white skin pulled taut over her cheekbones, likely caused by her hair twisted up into a knot on top of her head.

Chloe lifted the pecan pie up in her hands. "He's expecting this." By the woman's face and the way the two security guards standing to the side glanced her way, that was probably not the right thing to say. "I mean, yes, he's expecting me." So what if it was a little lie? He was expecting pie every week, and her statement was true enough.

The woman lifted a sleek black phone connected to a huge console of buttons, murmured a few things into it, and then set it back in the cradle. "Floor 9, Miss Hart."

Chloe entered the elevator with an elderly gentleman who stared into his phone. He pushed floor nine, her destination, and she settled herself against the back paneling.

As they rose, he pocketed his phone. "Smells good. Is it somebody's birthday or something?"

"Oh, no occasion. Do you know Nick Hollister?"

"I've heard the name. Lucky guy if he's getting his wife to deliver baked goods to his office." He lifted his chin toward her pie.

"Oh, I'm not his wife. But he is about to get very lucky." *Oh, my God.* She couldn't believe she'd said that. "I mean, it's lucky pie."

His eyebrows arched.

She quickly turned to face the elevator doors again, which was exactly where her gaze should have been the entire time.

When the elevator doors opened, he gestured for her to exit first. She did—and stepped straight into office hell.

A hushed thrum ran through the wide-open space full of gray fabric-lined cubicles. Office doors lined the opposing two walls, though they were like big glass squares with a door handle so anyone could peer inside to the inhabitants like zoo animals.

This firm certainly had some voyeuristic tendencies.

"This explains the tree limbs up everyone's butts the other night," she muttered. The industrial carpet smell alone nearly gagged her.

"Um, excuse me," she said to a woman in a—*shocker*—beige dress who was hurrying by. "Nick Hollister?"

It Was All The Pie's Fault

"Sixth door on the right." She at least smiled.

Chloe found his office easily as his voice rumbled down the hallway. It was accompanied by a female voice.

"I swear, Nick. It's the last time." The woman with long, shiny dark hair had a hold of Nick's arm.

He smiled down at her. "There will never be a last time with us and you know that. Anything you need at all, Maria…"

Their bodies mashed together in a hug. Anxiety and irritation prickled inside Chloe. Nick was hugging a woman named Maria who he'd do anything for. My, wasn't the man helpful?

And why was she feeling anything at all about this scene?

Chloe rapped on the door frame and they broke their embrace.

"Am I interrupting anything?"

Nick's face wore a puzzled expression. "Hi, Chloe. They said you were coming up."

"Oh, good. Delivery." She raised the pie in her hand.

The woman smiled at her. Nick did say men liked the hot ones—like the woman standing next to him. Dark eyes and long hair that curled down her back were just a couple of examples of this female's beauty.

She eyed Chloe, then eyed Nick.

"Come in." He tilted his chin in a gesture for her to enter.

Chloe didn't budge. "Sure I'm not intruding?"

His eyes narrowed, and then his lips inched up in amusement. "Mrs. Fernandez…" he swung his gaze her way, "I'd like to introduce you to Chloe Hart. She makes me pies."

The Fernandez case. "Oh, the—" Chloe stopped her words at Nick's stern face. *Right.* Chloe wasn't supposed to know anything about his cases.

She balanced the pie in one hand while she outstretched

the other. "It's very nice to meet you." Chloe was jumping to conclusions too easily these days.

Mrs. Fernandez returned her handshake. "Hello. That smells delicious."

"Pecan. Want some?"

"Oh, no, thank you." Mrs. Fernandez picked up her purse. "I must be going. Nick." She gave Nick a sly smile and scooted past.

When Chloe turned back to him, he leaned against his desk, wearing a lopsided smile, the bastard. "Looking a little green around the edges there."

He thought she was jealous? "It's not my color."

His smirk was uncalled for. She had been surprised at walking into his office to find himself glued to a woman, that was all.

"Uh-huh." He pushed off. "So, you're here. That's a surprise."

"I keep my promises." She lifted her pie.

He chuckled. "Come on, let's go to the kitchen. We both could use some sugar."

19

While she unwrapped the pie, Nick poured himself a cup of black coffee into a mug with the WSC logo scrolled on its side. "Tea?"

"No, thanks. I won't be staying long."

Chloe sighed and spun in a circle around the office kitchen. "I now understand why you don't believe in magic."

The tiny six-by-six-foot space with white cupboards, a sink, refrigerator, and a well-loved microwave was a tad depressing. But the design kept staff moving through it, not lounging about.

He peered over at her pie. "Fancy." She'd decorated the pie crust with a trophy cut-out and olive branches, all done in pastry dough. It was something he'd see in a high-end bakeshop. "Does this mean something?" With Chloe, nearly everything did.

"Pecan symbolizes wealth and financial security. I thought it appropriate given you are teaching me how to win."

"Ah, that explains the trophy." He pulled out two plates

from the shelf. "Speaking of winning, how is the man trap coming along?"

"The *rescue*. But I haven't seen Russell today. I'll have you know I'm skipping out on a meeting with him…" she reached into her bag sitting on the counter and glanced at her phone, "which is to start in five minutes. It's so not like me."

He ripped open a sugar packet. "So, who's watching the natives?"

"The who?"

He leaned against the counter. "Your students?"

"Oh, it's half-a-day all week." She pulled open a drawer—the wrong one for what he suspected she sought.

"Nice deal." He reached into a different drawer to a jangle of silverware, retrieved the pie server, and handed it to her.

She waved it at him. "Convenient to have this around."

"We have the obligatory birthday cakes once a quarter to celebrate everyone's at once."

"My, how very personal. No wonder everyone feels so… *special*." She fluttered her eyelashes and looked up at the ceiling.

He took a sip of scalding coffee. "Not meant to. It's meant to check a box." Despite WSC's commitment to work-life balance, they didn't like anything that encroached on normal work hours—whatever the hell they were.

"How efficient." She cut into the pie and placed a piece on his plate. "Okay, mister." She handed it to him. "Get ready with a new wish. What do you need to win next?"

A rustle of someone entering interrupted. "You did have a big one this morning. So, this beautiful lady is the reason, huh?" John, the one guy he liked in this place, leaned against the doorframe. Surprising he showed up given he rarely lifted his head from his desk. "Or the pie? Thought I smelled something."

Nick's neck and jaw tensed. "Pie's got nothing to do with

It Was All The Pie's Fault

this morning." Nick had closed on a discrimination settlement case earlier—straightforward. The win was not earned through some supernatural force or whatever mojo Chloe waved over her ingredients.

Chloe eyed John. "Nick doesn't believe in the magic." She plated another piece and handed it to him.

"There's nothing magic about hard work." Nick took a bite of pie. The pecan was fantastic—and so out of place here. Thanksgiving and Christmas memories flooded his mind. Had they served pecan pie before his stepfather screwed up his entire family? He couldn't quite grasp the thread in his mind.

John took a huge bite and immediately began nodding his head. After swallowing, he reached for a napkin. "There is certainly something magic about this pie. If only my wife baked." He dug in. "I'm John, by the way."

"Hi, John. I can give you the recipe." She cocked her hip, a move she was probably unaware was coquettish. If he knew anything about Chloe, she didn't recognize half her appealing quirks.

Nick wiped his mouth with the napkin. "You would share, huh? Thought your recipes were secret."

"Oh, Nana always said I should share if anyone asks. Sharing is a very important life skill."

"Chloe teaches first grade," Nick explained.

John stared at her a second too long. "That right?"

"You finish with that brief already?" The guy didn't need to hang around, and Nick knew the man was behind. Then again, were any of them ever ahead?

The man chuckled. "Yeah, well, share some of your good luck around, Nick." He eyed Chloe once more and finally sauntered off with his dessert.

"Another guy you don't like?" She leaned against the counter.

"I do." John was a talented attorney, and they were on fairly friendly terms. He just didn't like how his gaze lingered on Chloe.

Nick was about to take her arm and steer her back to the office when Mark Carter, an attorney in their family law practice and Hank Carter's nephew, conveniently appeared.

His eyes roamed all over Chloe. "Hello there."

"Hi." She smiled up at him. "I'm Chloe. Like pecan pie?"

"Love it." He once more glanced down at her breasts and then back up to her face with a look Nick did not like. Did not like at all.

A new intern, Jason, sauntered in. "Wow, something smells great."

Chloe immediately went to work cutting new pie pieces. "Okay, everyone. One bite of my pie and your wishes come true." She winked at Jason, who flushed as if he'd never seen a woman in his life.

"Is that right?" Mark glanced over at Nick and then resumed eyeballing Chloe.

"Yep." Chloe handed him a plate. "Only, Nick doesn't believe in my power."

Nick chuffed. "Oh, I believe, but I know where it comes from." He sidled closer to her to put some space between her and Mark and Jason.

Mark's reputation was the dead opposite of his father's. Hank Carter would have married a nun if it were allowed. Mark, however, was a walking one-night stand—actually, more like a few hours' stand.

"Magic pie." Mark smirked, his thoughts so transparent. He'd like to show Chloe some magic—no pie required. "I like it. So, I wish for a date—"

"I thought I smelled something good." Hank Carter elbowed his way inside, taking up the last inch of kitchen space. "I haven't had a good piece of pie since last Thanksgiving. Hello, Miss Hart."

They shook hands. "Hello, Mr. Carter. Care for some pecan?"

"Why, I think I will. Nick." He nodded at him.

She handed it over to him. "What do you wish for?"

Hank's eyebrows shot up. "Wish?"

Oh, Jesus. *There went the end of Nick's pretend-normal life.* "Chloe believes her pies are… special," he explained, and with any luck wouldn't need to explain further.

His boss took a bite and smiled down at her. He nodded once. "I believe they are. I'm going to miss these when you get to the L.A. office, Nick."

Yeah, he was too.

Mark licked the end of his fork, continuing to gape at Chloe. She really was a knockout in her own way. She wasn't trying. She was being normal, which, to a bunch of guys who only met women in bars, had to be a fresh take to them, the bonobos.

"We need to go." Nick grabbed her by the elbow to steer her away from this gaggle of testosterone. Dan's interest in her had been piqued. Mark looked like he wanted to take her into the supply closet and have his way with her. And who knows what went on in the head of Jason, a twenty-year-old bag of hormones. Whatever it was… *Not happening.*

20

"So, how was that in the flirting department? Did I pass?" she whispered as he steered her toward his office. She'd have to get her pan from him later.

He growled a little. "Yeah, I'd say you're good. But watch yourself, especially with Mark."

"He seemed nice enough." He sure seemed to like her pie, but then what's not to love? Slightly egotistic, but Nana's recipes were the best.

"Were you jealous?" She poked a finger in his side and he let out a low yip.

He put a little distance between them, the chicken. "Jesus, Chloe."

"Oh, you were." The way his eyes fired made her heart jump a little. He was kind of hot when he got all… well, hot and bothered. "I thought you could use the practice in chivalry. So you can *win* a woman someday. Like when you get to L.A. Land of the beautiful women." He needed someone who got him out of this depressing place now and again.

"I don't need practice in winning women," he grumbled.

Oh, please. "Are you always this arrogant when it comes to the female portion of the planet?"

He didn't answer.

She inched her purse strap up onto her shoulder. "I gotta get back. It's a teacher workday…" Her bag vibrated a little against her hip. She stopped short inside his office and reached for her phone.

"Oh, score again." She lifted her phone screen up to Nick's face.

<<Where are you? You okay?>>

He closed his hand over hers before she could answer it. "Do not answer that."

"Why not? Russell is wondering why I'm late to our meeting. I'll text him."

He snatched her phone from her.

"Hey." She jogged after him as he rounded to the other side of his office.

He flipped it over and read it.

"Gimmee," she nearly shouted.

"Listen, the point is to make him desperate for you. On second thought…" He started tapping a reply.

Her arms flailed toward him. "*Nick.* Give it back."

"God, you're cute when you get angry." He smiled and raised his arms so she couldn't reach it. "I won't send it. I'll show you what you should say." He handed it back to her.

She glared at him before glancing down at the message. "I'm with someone?" she parroted. "That's it?"

"That's it."

Her lips twisted. "This is downright childish."

"We're going for mystery."

Her phone buzzed. "Oh." She held it up so he could read it.

<<*Can you meet later? Maybe coffee? Pie?*>>

"Don't. Answer." He grasped her wrist. Jesus, this man

should have gone into the Marines by the way he was all "do this-don't do that."

"But, pie..." Russell would finally have some. How could Nick not see this as *the* development they were going after?

"No pie. Ignore it," he said. "Go back to school and go about your business. Trust me. It's too soon. You'll do this if you really want to make his attention last."

She huffed out a breath. "Okay."

"I'll pick you up. What time did you say?"

"Tonight I'm out at 9:30. I have parent-teacher conferences." She dropped her phone into her bag before he got any bright ideas to repossess it. "I was going to Uber home since your guy picked me up this morning."

"Good. That's about when I'd leave anyway. 9:30. Sharp."

She put her hands on her hips. "You really need to get out more, Nick. See how real people talk to one another."

"That's my wish for today's pie... to get out more." He sniggered. "But only if Hannity and Sons cave to my demands."

"Who are they?"

"Does it matter?"

She dropped her arms to her sides. "Are they the good guys or the bad guys?"

He looked down at the floor, laughed, and then glanced back up at her. He looked like he wanted to say something but then thought differently.

He eased her to his doorway. "We're the good guys. They are very, very bad..." He leaned forward, his cologne wafting over her. The intensity in his eyes was unwavering. He must *torch* his opponents—especially if they were women. Such a sexist thought, but there it was.

Crap. She should not be noticing such things about him—libido-type things.

"Consider your wish granted." She then pushed him back

a little in case his cologne had some other compliance-inducing properties—like making her put on another pencil skirt. She wouldn't put it past him.

"Chloe," his warning tone sounded. Yep, cinders and ash. That's what would be left of anyone he tried to beat.

"I promise. No messaging." She held up three fingers in the Girl Scout promise.

He grasped them for a quick second. "There's my girl."

21

After walking Chloe down to the lobby and seeing she got out without any more of his colleagues eye-fucking her, he headed back upstairs. Jesus, he was behind in his day now. Why did he offer to help her at all? Except she was so unguarded, guileless. Someone had to watch out for this woman.

Shit, she was getting under his skin. Women didn't get under his skin.

She was going to be bad for his business—at least getting work done. She turned out to be, however, stellar in the PR department.

As he headed back to his office, Hank Carter smiled at him in the hallway, an actual lifting of the lips that could even have been considered friendly. He thought for sure Chloe's confession about magic pie was going to be a black mark on his family-friendly, normal reputation. Law firms thrived off normalcy. Magic pies did not fit into the status quo. But maybe he'd dodged a bullet?

Then, another partner stopped by and congratulated him on his most recent win. It wasn't something they did often.

Nick dove back into work to drive a certain curvy woman from his head. Most notably, the image of her surrounded by a knot of men in a too-small kitchen wanting a taste of her pie—and probably more.

His neck soon ached, and his reflection grew increasingly sharper in his glass window as night fell outside. Man, he'd been lost in work. It was already 8:55. Time to get a move on. He hustled himself and his briefcase down the hallway and ran smack into Hank.

"Nick," he said with some ferocity.

This is where he was going to be chastised for bringing a crazy woman into the office, wasn't it?

"Glad to see things are moving along in the female department."

He laughed. Chloe would have laughed at that, too. "You mean Chloe. Yeah, sorry she distracted everyone today."

The man raised his hand. "No apology necessary. It was good for people to take a break."

Man, the work-life balance consultant really *had* gotten to the firm's partners.

"I've gotta run." Nick turned away but then turned back suddenly. "Gotta pick up Chloe from work."

The man smiled once more. The second one he'd earned from the guy today. *Huh.* Maybe Chloe was a little magic because Hank Carter only smiled when cases were won.

Nah. All the mumbo jumbo stuff was for movies and books.

Nick managed to make his way through traffic and arrive at Chloe's elementary school two minutes late. She wasn't outside. He parked and cracked open his door. He'd find her.

Only, she wasn't in her classroom, and the hallway was rather dark with only night-lights shining dim yellow circles to the polished floor every ten feet.

He texted her.

<<Where are you?>>

Three dots appeared and then disappeared. He did not get a good feeling about this.

Far-off voices echoed from down the hallway. He found her in the gymnasium—with Russell. Damn it, he'd told her to ignore the guy. Knowing her, she'd sought him out.

"Chloe." His voice bounced around the space. Nick closed the distance between her and Russell, who lifted his chin in acknowledgment.

"I was waiting for you out front," he said to her.

She glared at him a little and gritted her teeth. "In a second, okay?"

"I need a few minutes with Chloe," Russell said. "She'd got some new ideas we need to run through."

"I'd be happy to."

"No, she won't," Nick said. "We've got to go to that... thing, babe."

Her eyebrows shot up. Okay, even to him, the word 'babe' didn't trip off the tongue like lightning.

Russell eyed him, working his jaw like he couldn't quite make out what was happening. He glanced over at Chloe. "Tomorrow then. Suzette Marie is waiting anyway." Russell gave him a look—one he was quite familiar with. It conveyed, "*Top that.*"

Nick pulled Chloe into him. She grew rigid as a board. "See ya."

Russell blinked and shook his head a little but sauntered out. He glanced backward once, which was all Nick needed to go for phase two. He bent down and captured Chloe's mouth with his own.

Her hands shot up to his pecs.

He'd planned on making the kiss quick, something like a hello. But she was warm and soft in his arms, and his lips rather enjoyed the contact. If she'd have pushed him back,

It Was All The Pie's Fault

he'd have abandoned the kissing ship. Instead, she curled her hands into his jacket lapels, and what do you know, kissed him back with that fantastic ferocity she'd displayed the day Duke won.

When they finally broke from one another, she peered up at him with round and questioning eyes.

Russell had to be looking, but he couldn't tear his eyes from her face. Her skin was like cream and for once she wasn't hiding those adorable smattering of freckles dotting her nose.

She swallowed. "Why did you do that?"

Why had he? He was no impulsive teenager.

He released her fully, and her hands released their grip on his jacket.

"I need to get my stuff from my classroom," she blurted.

He followed her and tried hard not to stare at the sway of her hips in her sheath dress. He utterly failed in that department.

⁓

As soon as she was through her classroom door, she spun on him. "What's going on, Nick? You were jealous today and Russell made you jealous, too. That..." she waved her arm toward the hallway "thing you did wasn't an act."

"Thing?" He stepped closer. "You mean our second epic kiss?"

"Yes." She stepped backward, which only stirred some primal need to charge forth.

"Phase two. Show Russell what he's missing since he's blind to you."

"Blind?" She lifted her chin and pursed her lips. "He was looking for me today, remember?"

The animal part of him hardened to steel at her cute pout.

Her words, however, burned a little. Russell most definitely did not deserve this woman.

He scrubbed his hair and turned to sit down on one of the tiny desks. "I mean, he doesn't see the real you."

"Don't you sit on that." She pointed at the minuscule piece of furniture. "You'll crush it."

He chuckled. It was madness that he stood in a first grade classroom at all. "Yeah, I guess I've outgrown the child size." He moved toward her, and her sweet floral scent wafted up.

"I'd say." She crossed her arms, which caused that crease between her breasts to deepen.

Maybe he'd been wrong about tamping down her schoolmarm look because it was hot as fuck. "You kissed me back."

She blinked at the sudden change in subject. "I did not."

Oh, yes, she had.

"Take it back." She poked at his chest.

He chuckled.

She jabbed him once more. "I mean it."

"Hey. Stop." He grabbed her hand, soft as butter. He curled his fingers around her wrist and pulled her closer to him.

Her throat moved in a delicate swallow. "Don't kiss me again, okay?" Her voice wavered.

His heart thudded more than it should have. Like it had when she'd cried over Russell after Chad's basketball party.

Shit. What was he doing? He wasn't sure what had come over him back in the gym. He dropped her hand and stepped backward. "Got it."

She twisted away and gathered her things. "I'm ready to go."

He was, too. His momentary lapse in judgment was over. Time to get her home.

They drove to her place in silence, the ticking of his directional signal the only sound in the car. He should say something. Hell, apologize at least. He was here to turn her over to another man, and he didn't break his promises. He also didn't launch himself at women. He had crossed a line with that kiss, which was so not like him.

His brakes hissed a bit as he stopped before her apartment's front entrance.

She cracked open the door. "See you."

"Yes. Friday. 4:30 p.m. For the wine and cheese. Remember, the white lace dress." Why did those words sound all wrong? She clearly didn't want his attentions—and he shouldn't want to be giving them. He was moving in a few months, for Christ's sake, and she would stay here.

She didn't look at him. "I will. But because I promised I would. So Russell can see it."

Yeah, nothing was getting her out of Moors-fucking-boresville. He, however, couldn't get himself, Daphne, and his nephew to the West Coast fast enough. Especially now.

22

"Over here," Chloe called to the two burly guys. Their biceps strained their Davidson & Sons T-shirts as they maneuvered two plywood trees into position.

Thank goodness for parents who owned construction companies. The makeshift landscaping for the spring fling's backdrop only needed to be painted. Then, voila! They'd have a magical forest for her first graders to frolic in.

She glanced at her clipboard. So far, the magical forest creatures—her students—included three unicorns, four fairies, a fireman, two cowboys, and an elephant. If only the parents of her students showed as much enthusiasm for helping their kids with their letters as they did the costumes. Of course, costumes meant shopping, so...

She shook that cynical thought from her head. Nick was rubbing off on her, wasn't he? When he wasn't *kissing her*.

Drat it all. She'd been trying to rub his face from her mind for the last twenty-four hours. She'd dreamed of him kissing her, touching her, pressing her down into her mattress.

Then he had to go send flowers—a gigantic bouquet of daisies and peach roses. The front desk aide delivered it to

It Was All The Pie's Fault

her classroom, which only caused her students to question her like mad for five minutes. They didn't grow six year olds like they used to. The modern kids missed nothing.

Nick didn't, either. He must have identified daisies were her favorite flowers from the print on her bed comforter.

Crapplo. There went the image of him sprawled on her bed assessing her body. Her *clothes*, she mentally corrected.

She set her clipboard down and kneeled before six paint trays set up over tarps.

"Hey." Russell's voice was a welcome interruption.

She rose. "Hey." She hadn't expected to see him today. "I thought you'd be home packing. You leave tomorrow for Paris, right?"

"Not going. Markinson thinks it will send the wrong message to parents as word has spread about me and Suzette Marie."

Oooh, smutty times blocked by the principal. Give the man a raise. "I'm sorry." She wasn't—at all. "I didn't know about you and Suzette Marie…"

"Eh. It'll be a matter of time."

Seems like arrogance wasn't only for one bossy attorney named Nick. It chafed her insides a bit, like he could snap his fingers and make anything happen he wanted. Even her magic didn't work that way. Both parties had to agree, even somewhat, and it be for the larger good. "Doesn't she get a say?" She meant for it to come out light, like a half-laugh.

His beautiful blue eyes fixed on her face and his jaw hardened. "So, Nick…" He scratched his chin. "He's treating you well? Things okay there?"

Oh, for crikey's sake. Even Russell was mentioning him?

"Fine. Fine." She waved her hand.

Russell captured her wrist. *Oh*. That stopped everything. Everything except her heartbeat, which pounded like an out-of-control drummer.

"You sure?" His brows furrowed. "I mean, you seem off this week."

His concern was palpable. She could use this. She could inject a little hesitation about Nick, give him an opportunity to swoop in.

"Things are complicated." Not a lie. "Maybe you could help there."

Russell let go of her. "They usually are where Nick is involved."

A prickly sensation bloomed over her chest. "What do you mean?"

"I've known the guy for a while. He's been known to lead a girl on and then ghost them when he's done."

That didn't sound like Nick to her. "That right?" It actually sounded like something Russell would do.

"Yeah. Be careful, okay? You've clearly captured his attention, but…" He shrugged.

But what? She wasn't enough to interest someone like Nick? She opened her mouth to say something when his attention was caught by two boys pushing each other on the bleachers. "Jared. Dean. Over here."

The two boys groaned and sulked over. It was time for her to get back to work anyway. Those trees weren't painting themselves, and she needed to think about this strange encounter—the second one with Russell this week.

"Call me anytime, Chloe. If you want to… talk." He turned away. "Now, you two… grab a paintbrush. Time to help Miss Hart." Little crinkles formed around his eyes. "I'm helping, too."

He wanted to help. Prior irritation—gone. *Because touchdown.* Maybe he was jealous, and he felt he *had* to keep his options open, too. After all, she'd flaunted Nick in front of him. Things really *were* complicated.

She knelt down and grasped two brand new paint-

It Was All The Pie's Fault

brushes. "Russell, mind getting them started? I have to make a quick call."

"Sure. Anything, Chloe."

She swiftly moved into the hallway and pulled out her phone. She had to report this news. Russell wasn't going to Paris. He'd started worrying about her. He was staying to paint. That last one was at least a touchdown, if not more. She also needed a little interpretation help.

<<Thanks for the flowers. And guess what?>>

Those maddening three dots appeared showing he was typing—and then they vanished.

Huh.

<<Russell is helping me today. *Voluntarily.* Score one for the Nick School of Men.>>

She waited a few minutes. Nothing. He was at work, so what could she expect?

With a happy heart, she skipped back to the gymnasium.

Russell ended up sticking around all afternoon to help her with the set painting. He kept glancing her way and tried to talk more about Nick—the one topic she'd not wanted to discuss at all. In fact, the more she ignored Russell, the more he tried to engage her.

She brought up Suzette Marie to test his newfound interest, but he deflected that topic with a wave of his hand. It miffed Chloe he dismissed her so easily.

At the end of the day, he walked her to the car service Nick had sent.

When the driver made a move to open the car door, Russell chuffed and stepped between her and the driver to open it for her.

"So, thanks for the help today," she said to him, her hands curled over the open door's edge.

He leaned over and kissed her on the cheek. "Anything to help. And I like this new look on you, by the way."

Her breath caught. Right then, she should have been over the moon with joy, but her happy mood was more like Swiss cheese. Sort of there and sort of *not*.

"Nothing new. Just me," she tittered, then slipped inside.

He closed her door and waved once as the black sedan pulled from the curb.

As soon as they exited the parking lot, the whole scenario seemed ridiculous. She'd gotten Russell's attention alright, but she'd had to *plan* for it. Like one of her school projects.

When she got home, after she'd washed the paint out of her hair and from under her fingernails, she tried yet another text to Nick.

<<Can we talk?>>

She wanted to hear his voice, get his take on things even if she was going to have to now entertain Nick might have been right all along about Russell. He wasn't exactly who she thought he was. He enjoyed being lured.

She finally got a reply from him.

<< Friday.>>

Oh, he did have a bad day. She could feel it.

<<Want to see the bodalicious outfit? Just to check?>>

Nothing came back. The night dragged on and still no answer. Outer space was louder than the message he was obviously sending. He didn't want to talk to her. Something wasn't right at all.

23
———

Chloe scratched a little at the lace at her neckline. The conference room was hot like a greenhouse. The room was crammed with suited men, and women gave each other tight smiles and clutched their plastic cups like they were having to try to have fun. Thank God she'd put brandy in the apple pies she brought.

"That's brilliant," a woman in black exclaimed.

A woman in champagne beige nodded in agreement. "I'll try that angle next time."

For thirty minutes, Chloe had been fingering her warm plastic wine glass of chardonnay, listening to the female colleagues hang on Nick's every word as he regaled them of his approach to a case.

Something about evoking *whistleblower rights* and *constructive discharge*—all Greek to her.

He'd sent a car to come get her that afternoon as he had every morning and afternoon since *the kiss*. She'd stopped bothering to text him, believing they could act like adults and talk tonight. But he hustled her to the gathering as soon as she stepped off the elevator. She'd asked for a few minutes, but he said, "No time." He didn't seem to want to talk to her at all.

He also didn't touch either of her two apple pies. She'd made one for him to take and another for this little shindig. Only, he told her to set them both out.

Maybe he felt as awkward as she did about him kissing her? Or didn't know what to say? She didn't either.

Like, how about she couldn't stop thinking about him and his kiss? He had to be good at that, too? Right now, three days later, she could conjure up how firm his lips were, how warm his chest was against her, and how she'd felt sheltered against his large body. She'd wanted to disappear inside his arms.

These thoughts were not like her at all. Or they shouldn't be given how much their plan for her to get Russell back was working. The man had stopped by her classroom twice today with some silly update on the show, something that could have waited until their next meeting. And he was always there in the mornings when she arrived as if he was looking for her. He seemed relieved a car service was dropping her off—and not Nick.

All of this should have her jumping up and down with glee. Instead, she couldn't get her bearings like she was riding a perpetual seesaw.

"Wow, this is good," a male voice said behind her. "I'm sorry I missed this from the other day."

"Chloe." Nick's hand tightened on her waist as they turned together to find a man devouring a piece of her pie. "You remember John Hammond from the other day."

At least Nick appeared happy to see this guy. John chewed, swallowed, and held out his hand. "Good to see you again." He pointed down at his plate. "This is magic."

"My, how word has gotten around," Nick said.

It Was All The Pie's Fault

"Next time, warn a guy when this..." he lifted his plate, "walks back into the place."

Nick frowned.

"Get in line, Hammond." Mark Carter joined them. His arm circled around a girl with hair too blond for her skin tone.

Chloe tamped down her disparaging thoughts. After all, she herself wore a cocktail dress that was, quite frankly, too tight.

"That wishing thing. Not so bad." Mark peered over at his date. "Met this lovely young thing that night over at Shockers."

Chloe must have looked puzzled because Nick leaned down and whispered. "Sports bar. Down the street."

Chloe nodded. "Ooooh."

John smacked his lips. "Hey, by the way, not to mix business with pleasure, but Hannity called. Wants to set up a meeting. Looks like you've gotten to them." John scooped the final bite of pie into his mouth.

Chloe raised her eyebrows toward Nick in an "oh, really" gesture.

Nick ignored her. "We'll close ranks first thing Monday."

He laughed. "What? No Saturday emergency meeting?"

"It can wait until Monday. Make them sweat it out."

John shrugged. "Your case."

The group dispersed and Chloe squared herself to Nick. "So, winning again, Mr. Hollister?"

He murmured.

"Looks like Mark's wish got granted," she whispered and looked over at Mark. "He got a date."

"Mark's always got a date. Or, should I say hookup. Let's go." He grasped her hand. "We need to talk."

Finally.

Once inside his office, Nick threw himself into his chair.

Dark circles colored under his eyes and his shoulders hunched over a bit. Clearly, it had been a long week for both of them. Her own eyelids were feeling a little heavy.

She strode to the window overlooking the city below. Her reflection was sharp in the glass, almost presenting itself as if she stared into a mirror. "It's so quiet in here."

"Yeah, perks of being at the opposite end of the building from the whine and schmooze show."

She glanced around at his office. It contained a typical desk and executive chair with a pastoral-scene painting hanging on the wall behind him. She'd seen that picture somewhere before, which meant it was mass-produced, impersonal. The entire space was downright sad. "If you hate those things so much, why go?"

"My presence is expected."

"Do you always do what's expected of you?" she chided.

"Probably." He thunked his chair to the upright position and fingered a pen that'd been lying on his ink blotter. "But you made them more fun. You certainly had everybody's attention tonight." He didn't sound happy.

Maybe it was the dress. She smoothed down the lace and stared at her reflection in the window. "I never thought this dress would look that good."

"It's amazing, and I'd say it was more than the dress."

She turned to him. "My pie?"

His eyes remained downcast. "More."

She perched herself on the edge of the desk and gave his shoe a soft kick with her toe. "That's because you're good. We need to talk about the other night, but want to start by telling me what's wrong?"

He finally lifted his gaze to her. "Nothing's wrong."

Uh-huh. "I'd say you're impressing your colleagues. They like you. You should hang out with them more. I mean, socially."

One side of his mouth quirked. "Let's not get carried away."

She leaned down to him. "Don't you ever get carried away?" She winked.

"I knew you could wink." His eyes glanced at her cleavage.

Oops. She righted herself. "I'd say you got carried away the other night." Her words slipped right out. Nana had said the longer you denied the truth, the more it wanted to come out. She'd been right.

He rested his head against the back of his chair. "Yeah, about the other night. Sorry. I'm usually a consent kind of guy. And now that Russell is putty in your hands..."

She wouldn't say *putty*. "More like play-doh. So now, I guess we can... lay off a bit."

He rose as well and immediately towered over her. "Lay off?" His hawk-like eyes focused down at her—actually, at her lips.

"We should stop. I mean, it's getting... weird." Like how she couldn't stop thinking about Nick when she needed to be thinking about Russell. "You're moving soon."

"In a few months, yes."

"And things between us are getting confusing."

"Confusing, huh?" He inched closer. "You mean like how you like my attention after all?"

What an arrogant... Maybe Russell had been right. "I wouldn't say that."

"Oh? What would you say?"

Telling him the truth would be humiliating. She sat on the edge of the desk. Mere inches separated them. "It's just... I should be thinking about Russell and only Russell."

"You're not?" One eyebrow raised in smug amusement.

She stood up and turned away. "Of course, I am." Her heartbeat thumped against her ribs.

He was behind her in seconds, and he turned her to face him. Her hand landed on his pec.

"So bossy." She should push him away to get some space. Instead, she drummed her fingers a bit and he chuckled.

His hand closed over hers—engulfed it, actually. "I have rather enjoyed making old Russ jealous."

She supposed he'd been right. Jealousy had worked. But did she want a guy who only wanted her when another might step in? But then, did she want to have her head filled with a guy like Nick who had no interest in love? And he was moving. In fact, he couldn't get out of the town she loved fast enough.

"You certainly have made him wonder," she said. "Like why are you with someone like me?"

His cheeks dropped a little. "You think too little of yourself." He tucked a strand of hair behind her ear, the gentle touch of his finger on the shell of her ear lighting up places inside her that should stay dark.

She should push away from him. "It's not that. I'm thinking too much…"

"Of?"

She looked up at him. "You." Stupid truth bomb.

"Is that bad?" His chest breached the last space between them, and her breasts were now mashed against him. Her nipples poked through her bra as if seeking more contact.

"Are you going to kiss me again?" If he did, she'd not be able to resist. She knew that much about herself. It was like eating a perfect pie. One piece was never enough.

He shook his head. "No."

Her hips pressed against the back of the desk as he leaned her further back. "Good. Because if you did—"

"What?" His hands landed on the desk on either side of her hips. His lips were perilously close to hers.

"I might not want you to stop."

His gaze turned feral, locked onto her face as if daring her to turn away. "Tell me to stop, then."

She could. In fact, she should. Isn't that what she taught all day? Impulse control? Then again, her body vibrated with a banked, primal need that wasn't denied easily.

She slowly shook her head, once, twice. "I don't want to stop."

His fingers cradled her chin. "Me either."

His fingers tightened on her jawline and his lips took possession of her mouth. His arms were next, banding around her, pulling her up to him. The room spun around and her back met the wall, the edge of a picture frame digging into her back.

Strong fingers traveled down to her hemline and yanked the fabric higher on her thighs. And when his hardness found the valley between her legs, a long sigh left her body and was lost in his mouth.

Frantically, his hand circled her leg and yanked her knee up so he could nestle his thickness right where she needed it. The wicked man pressed himself against her—just enough to make her desperate for more.

Oh, God, he could move his tongue around. She'd never believed herself to be that good at kissing. Nick, however, was a master. Or maybe it's because they just seemed to fit.

Her inner thighs throbbed in response.

"Chloe," he breathed into her mouth like an oath. "What are you doing to me?"

To him? He was melting her. Her mind, her scruples, her resistance was liquefying to the ground.

He broke his hold on her mouth and kissed her cheek, down her neck to her cleavage. His hand engulfed her breast and he squeezed. "Mine."

Oh, wow. She'd never gone for possessive guys before and

now she wondered why not because *hot*. Her leg hitched higher and her hands tunneled into his thick hair.

"I need to kiss you everywhere." He fell to his knees in front of her and pushed up her dress until it was a mass of lace and liner scrunched around her waist. She'd worn white lace panties to match the dress—not that she'd have believed anyone would have seen them.

Nick now saw everything. His dark eyes glinted up at her. "You are so fucking hot."

She vigorously shook her head. She wasn't hot. She was a schoolteacher. She baked. She wasn't...

Oh, God, he hitched her leg over his shoulder and inhaled deeply.

"You have no idea how hard you make me with your prim and proper schoolmarm act."

"It's not an act," she breathed out.

He chuckled. "Even better." His face pressed against her panty-covered sex as his fingers cradled the plushest part of her ass. His mouth went straight for where she *throbbed*. Like, so hard, she could almost hear it pulsing.

Her fingers dug deeper into his scalp as he went at her with his tongue and lips. Pleasure sparkled through her entire body, and she had to curl her lips in on her teeth so she didn't cry out too loudly.

Her blood turned to honey but still throbbed through her limbs, which had turned to melted butter. The wildness grew as his confident tongue swiped and dug into the fabric barring him from full access. He licked ruthlessly, and when he adjusted her leg on his shoulder, he hit that magic spot.

She came so hard against his face, she nearly bucked off the wall, but his hands held her fast.

Her fingers dug into his hair and she gulped in air. She set her head back against the painting. The stupid thing had to be bolted onto the wall given her movements. She tried to catch her breath.

He rose slowly, his body blocking out the fluorescent lights above. Her head turned away to catch their reflection in the glass. He followed her gaze.

"So. Hot," he panted as their eyes locked in the mirrored glass.

Two men's laughter sounded in the hallway, which was all it took for panic to settle in.

What the hell was she doing? She pushed her dress down frantically.

Nick stood back, wiping his mouth. "Don't worry about them."

She blinked. "Don't *worry*?"

Record scratch. Worry rushed in like a tsunami. She came all over Nick Hollister's face—the man who was trying to help her reconnect with another man. She was going to call off their whole deal and now he'd... he'd... She couldn't even think it.

Oh, God, what had she done?

"Chloe." Nick's warning tone really irritated.

"I need a ladies' room."

He nodded once and pointed to the door. "On the left at the end of the hall."

She grasped her bag and coat. "Can you call a car service for me?"

"I'll take you home."

"No." She straightened. "A car service, please." She had to stop this madness.

He pursed his lips but nodded.

24

Chloe sipped her coffee and dawdled her fork in the pan. Brownies had eggs and milk, so as far as she was concerned, the chocolate goodness was breakfast food.

She peered into her oven. She had four pies baking for Greta at Peppermint Sweet. Ten more minutes should do it.

She pushed back from the counter and sighed. She hadn't gotten out of her PJs yet. She'd needed to be close to her Nana, and they were the last gift she'd given her. Little pie icons and a waft of steam rising above each one dotted the soft blue flannel.

She didn't feel like baking, but Greta had asked if she could drop off more of her death-by-chocolate, cherry, and pineapple-mango pies soon. The thought made her heart cave in a little. Nick loved cherry.

Nick Hollister. The frickin' nerve of the man and his wicked tongue.

Last night was a disaster. Come to think of it, the last few weeks had been one thing after the other.

"Let's recap," she said into the brownie pan.

It Was All The Pie's Fault

First, Nick helped launch her pie into Russell's lap. "The one guy I was trying to impress." She waved her fork. "Which gave Russell permission to pursue Suzette Marie, who doesn't even friggin' want him." Like Russell listened to her? Not. He tried to finagle a way to Paris to get closer to her. "He should be taking *me* to Paris."

She then struck a devil's deal with the jaded attorney who didn't believe in her magic. "He is so missing out."

She continued to prostrate herself in front of said attorney with more pies. Sure, the other guys in his office seemed to appreciate her baking. But given that depressing office? "They'd appreciate Twinkies picked up at 7-11."

The brownie pan was a good listener.

"Then? To top it off?" Russell's attention was magically secured, but she wasn't quite sure how she felt about it. He was pursuing Suzette Marie, and now, he seemed to want Chloe, as well?

"Nick had been right about him." *Then there was more. Freaking more* ridiculousness in the form of last night's smutty shenanigans. After Nick promised her there wouldn't be any.

Wait. Had he promised? Or had she just declared it?

Gah. Whatever it was… "He should not have gone there." And then, to be so spectacular at said shenanigans? Unconscionable.

She squeezed her thighs together at the memory of his lips and the way his hands grabbed fistfuls of her thighs like he couldn't get enough of her.

She pushed her pan friend away. Before she knew it, she'd be scrawling Nick's name in the margins of her kids' lesson plans and sexting him while her kids did their art projects.

Okay. She had to use her brain. She needed a pro and con list.

Russell was stable, charming, and wanted a life very similar to what she wanted—family, little house in the suburbs. He also was pushy, fickle, and, quite frankly, had a sarcastic judgmental streak she'd not noticed before.

Nick was smart, sometimes charming, and had things he could do with his mouth that she could never forget. He was also pushy, fickle, and, quite frankly, had a sarcastic judgmental streak she'd *always* noticed.

But therein lay an answer. She'd noticed Nick's characteristics immediately, and with Russell, she'd been as blind as a blind bat in an underground cavern—and not one of the cool ones with stalagmites and stalactites and pretty crystals winking at her.

A loud buzz went off, and she nearly jumped out of her PJs. Five more minutes showed on the timer. Another buzz sounded. Oh, the doorbell.

"And on top of it all, I am losing my mind."

She opened the door, forgetting she was still in her loungewear. "Russell?" She blinked and clutched her lapels.

"You've had a long week. Caffeine?" He lifted two paper cups with "Peppermint Sweet" on the side. "Coffee black, right?"

"Tea. But…" She stepped backward and let him in. "What are you doing here?"

"Checking on you." He strode inside. "Wow, what smells amazing? What are you cooking?"

"Baking. Um… pie?" Did this man have a mental block about her pie baking? She shook her head. "Russell, aren't you sending Suzette Marie off today? I mean, today was the day they were leaving, right?"

"Nah. Things aren't going to work out."

Suzette Marie dashed his hopes, hadn't she? Score one for Suzette Marie. She was clearly smarter and faster about men than Chloe could ever be.

"I wanted to see you." He ran his hand down her arm, and gooseflesh raised all the hairs on her body. Now that Russell stood in her apartment—for the first time—she didn't really want him here.

He set the coffee down on her counter and strode to the oven, peering in. "What kind? I'm hungry." He peeled off his coat.

She rubbed her arm where he'd touched her. "They're for Peppermint Sweet. Listen. One second."

She didn't wait for his answer but went in search of real clothes.

While she was pulling on jeans, the oven door squeaked in the kitchen. What was he doing?

She jogged back to the kitchen area and heard the timer had gone off. "I've got these." She grabbed oven mitts and reached inside to pull them out.

"Okay." He scrunched his lips. "Those brownies look good." He picked up her fork and dug in as she pulled out her pies one by one. Russell's fork scraped against the pan.

After setting a pie on each of the stove's burners, she moved to get him a plate. That scraping sound would raise the dead.

She unwound the ribbon that she tied around both handles of her kitchen cabinet doors to keep them shut. After retrieving a plate, she set it before him. "Here."

He smiled. He'd casually draped his coat over the back of her stool. Looks like he came over to stay for a bit.

She picked up one of the coffees and took a sip to be polite. *Ick.* "Russell? Why are you really here?"

He dabbed his lips with a napkin. "I'm worried. Something's up with you. You're... different." His annoyance was clear.

"Different's not bad." She winked. Jesus, see what Nick did to her? Involuntary eye spasms were now de rigueur.

"Don't get me wrong." He raised a hand. "You look good, but something is off. I'm not sure Nick is good for you. I mean, his influence—"

"Is what?" Two short sharp words that she'd like an answer to.

"I mean, I like the changes, but you're not like this."

They didn't speak for a few long seconds. She wasn't being herself? She supposed he wasn't entirely wrong on that account given Nick's coaching, yet she didn't feel like a different person, either. More like she'd opened up to parts of herself she rarely let out.

Yeah, like a woman who hiked up her skirt in offices...

She leaned her forearms on the counter and peered over her cup. "Or maybe this is who I was all along."

"I know you. And this..." he waved his hand at her, "isn't you."

She straightened. "Maybe it is."

He smirked. "Nah."

Before full-on irritation could take hold, he moved around the island. He glanced over her shoulder. "I can fix that for you." She spun to face her cabinet door that hung open.

"I could go get some tools. Do it now." He drew closer to her.

His blue eyes were exquisite—so perfect, almost unreal. But also, they were flat and distant. Scarlett had asked what she'd seen in Russell, and right now? She couldn't think of a single thing.

A shudder racked her whole body. "I have pies to deliver today."

His hands rested on her shoulders. "Okay, how about tomorrow?"

She glanced down at his hands, so much smaller than

Nick's and, she could tell even without the skin-to-skin contact, softer.

"Chloe."

She would have done anything a few weeks ago to have him stare at her like he was doing now. Something had shifted inside her. "Yes?" She wouldn't mind hearing the words, though.

"Maybe I didn't really give us a chance because now..." He leaned down, and his lips met hers. She gasped into his mouth, so not ready for this development. He moved his lips and his tongue darted in, a hot, fleshy slice that had her stumble backward.

The kiss was... disgusting.

She jerked backward, needing some distance from him. "But Suzette Marie. You seemed so into her."

He inched one shoulder up. "We're here. She's there."

When he moved forward again, her arms jutted out to fend him off. He paused and cocked his head. She grabbed the counter to steady herself, but her hand landed in the brownie pan.

A smile formed on his face, a little sinister, a little smarmy now that she really looked at him. He reached for her like he wanted to kiss her again.

Whoa... Her reactions kicked in. Her fingers curled around the edge of the brownie pan and she smacked him in the shoulder with it. Brownie bits flew and one giant L-shaped chunk dropped to their feet, hitting both her slippers and his shoes.

"Ow." He grasped his arm. "What was that?" He stepped backward and shook brownie off one foot. "A simple 'no' would have sufficed."

"How about asking for a 'yes' first?" Since he didn't, she clung to the pan just in case he got any more ideas. Thank God she owned heavy-duty bakeware.

What was with it with these men who believed they could launch themselves at her? For once in her life, she was popular, and this was how it manifested itself?

Her doorbell went off. She jogged to the door and yanked it open.

"Hey." Nick lifted up two paper cups with Peppermint Sweet's logo nearly disappearing behind his large hands. "Tea?"

"Oh, thank God." She grasped his arm and pulled him in.

"Hey, hey." He bent over as if steadying the drinks in his hand. "Careful."

He straightened when he caught sight of Russell, one hand on the kitchen island, the other brushing brownie off his shoes. He glanced down at Chloe, then to the pie pan she now had across her chest like armor—a very messy, gooey shield.

"Everything okay?"

"Yes. I'm baking. It... slipped." Why had she lied?

One side of his mouth inched up. "Someone's wish go awry?" His face hardened as he glanced back up at Russell. "Or..." He stepped deeper inside. "Thought you were going to Paris."

"Tell that to the puritanical mob known as the PTA." He stood straight and stretched his back casually as if he hadn't just tried to kiss her. Heck, *grope* her.

She strode to the counter and dropped her pan weapon with a loud clang. Bits of brown goo were stuck to her chest but she could care less.

Nick set the cups down on the counter, instantly noticing the other coffees sitting there. "Suzette give you the boot?"

Russell's eyes fired. "Hardly."

What was this strangeness? She eased her grip off Nick's arm, something she hadn't realized she'd been doing.

"You know what?" She waved at her pies. "I really need to deliver these." And take a moment—or one hundred—to sort through the Twilight Zone-worthy things that have happened in the last twenty-four hours. She grasped a towel and went to the sink, brushing off brownie crumbs into the basin.

"I'll take you," Russell said.

"No need, my man. I've got it." Nick glanced at her and then back at Russell. "It's why I'm here. What I can't get my head around is why *you* are here."

"I was worried about Chloe, to be honest."

Chloe opened her mouth to speak, but Nick filled in for her. "She's fine."

"So she keeps telling me. But I know Chloe. She's not." Russell surveyed him. "Something's off."

"But nothing."

"Oh, I'd say it's something."

"Guys." Chloe dropped the towel on the counter and held up her hands. "I don't know what's going on here, but please..." Please what? Stop fighting over her? Or rather, stop fighting over them both trying to one-up one another.

That's what this was about, wasn't it? It wouldn't matter if it were her or any other woman. My, how wrong she'd been about this whole scenario.

She suddenly felt badly for Suzette Marie—the prize in the room that everyone just wanted to win.

No more, at least when it came to her.

Russell eyed one of the cherry pies. "Hey, Chloe, how about I buy one of those pies from you right now?"

Fingers of excitement should have rushed up at the thought of Russell eating a piece of the cherry pie. Instead... no pie for Russell Montgomery Langston.

She didn't want him.

Wow. Her desire for him... vanished. Russell was a project when, really, what she wanted was a partner. Someone like Nick. Someone who worked with her—not someone she had to *work*.

"Sorry." She looked over at Nick. "The pies are spoken for already."

His eyes lit up with pride. Her heart flipped over, and suddenly, she felt lighter as if freed from being trapped under a truckload of anvils. Nick was a partner—*her* partner.

Russell pursed his lips and nodded. "I see they are." He grasped his coat and stomped to the door. He paused in the doorway. "Later, Chloe."

As soon as Russell was through the door, Nick turned to her. "Touchdown indeed. I'd say you've made headway with Russell. He was pissed-off jealous I was here. That's the best kind." His eyes slanted downward. "Now tell me jealousy doesn't work."

"Yeah, about that..."

He held up his hand. "First, are you okay?"

His concern was touching. "I'm fine. It was... nothing." She bent down and retrieved another piece of brownie from the floor and tossed it into the sink.

"Well, then let me say a few things. I came to apologize. I got out of hand last night. Second time, too."

The truth was, she'd liked it. More than liked it. "You didn't overstep, I mean—"

"You're safe with me. I promise. It's important to me you know that."

She studied Nick's handsome face. He was more than what he portrayed at first blush. He was honest—and kind. He was exactly who she thought Russell was on the inside. It was as if her mind had flipped their characters, their true selves.

She stepped toward him. "You don't have to apologize. It takes two to tango."

"Oh, I'd say we did more than tango."

His smile was genuine—albeit a little on the cocky side. But he had reason to be. Nick was better than Russell.

She closed the distance between them. "Want to do it again?"

25

Chloe's lips twisted and she stared at his mouth. She was serious.

"But Russell…"

"I can do better." Her voice was breathy.

He grasped her chin. "So, I was right."

Silence spread between them.

"You can't say it, can you?" That she'd discovered she didn't want Russell, like he thought. Damn, his skin nearly burst with his swollen ego on that one.

"I can." She rose up on tiptoes, put her hands on his shoulders, and pressed her lips to his. Words were overrated anyway—especially when she kissed as she did.

Her mouth connected with his, and *damn*.

His pie queen, the woman who believed in magic and fairytales and didn't want to wear an "eff me outfit," certainly knew how to call up nothing but effing with her lips. All his body could think about was how fast he could settle between her thighs, feel her bare skin.

When she broke her kiss, he stared down at her. "But, Chloe—"

It Was All The Pie's Fault

"I don't want Russell. I want you."

Him. He touched his lip, a little stunned, actually. Sure, he'd been right about Russell, but this turn of events was more than he could have hoped for—and he hadn't hoped for anything.

Still, who was he to question his good fortune?

He grabbed her glorious butt as he kissed her, deep and hard. He lifted her up and she yelped into his mouth.

He set her up onto the counter, sending the brownie pan clattering to the floor.

She broke their kiss. "Hey, caveman."

"I haven't gotten you to the cave yet, and when I do—"

"Yes?" Little flecks of gold sparkled in her eyes.

Oh, the things that tumbled into his mind would shock Lucifer. "Lots of... stuff."

Her pretty pink lips moved up into a smile so wicked and seductive his most basic self took over. He yanked her knees wider apart. "What happened to no shenanigans?"

"You're a good attorney. Revise the contract."

His smart woman. He tucked a piece of hair behind her ear. "Why, Chloe Hart... you're making me blush."

Her hands went to his belt buckle, and swear to God, he nearly did blush if it hadn't been for the fact he was too busy ridding her of clothes. Getting her nude turned out to be easy. No protest. No timid virginal protests. She kicked off her jeans and pulled her top over her head.

His belt was undone, and before they got any further, he got her to the bedroom. She'd clung to him as he moved them through her apartment. Shedding the rest of his clothes with her help, they sent a few buttons skittering across the floor and left some items turned inside out, but who could pay attention to such matters for long? Not when Chloe, nude on her daisy comforter, shone her eyes up at him full of want and mischief.

Somehow, he got a condom on in no time as the little vixen had them in her nightstand. Why did he believe he knew anything about this woman?

She pulled him down to her. Soft hands trailed his back as their teeth grazed each other. Finding her heat and entering her was so sweet, he yanked her thigh higher on his hip so he could go deeper.

He'd never been a fan of kissing—all that sloppy wet traded back and forth. But she'd revised his thoughts on that a while ago. She tasted of coffee and chocolate, and moans rumbled in her throat that he swore he could feel in his chest.

His weight had her pinned to the bed, and he ground into her, earning little mewls. They grew louder. Chloe was so unselfconscious, so freed, he flipped her over to take her from behind. He needed to see that gorgeous ass move as he thrust into her.

He banded his arm around her waist and worked her with his fingers. That's when loud grew into long keens and pants that made him hold off releasing until she did. His forehead fell to her shoulder as she shuddered underneath him.

Finally, he could let go. Sweat had broken out along his brow from his delaying tactics but was so worth feeling her clench against him. His own orgasm nearly took his head off.

They fell side by side, him caging her from behind. She stretched out her legs in front of her and purred. "Mmmm."

She then twisted to face him. Her hand cradled his cheek, her finger tracing his lower lip. "Okay. You were right. About—"

"You being bodalicious. Yes, I was." He couldn't hear her confession after what's-his-name. He couldn't hear that guy's name on her tongue—not after all the things he'd done with said tongue. He ran his hand along her side, loving how his palm dipped down and back up the slope of her hip. "I'm always right."

She pushed on his shoulder. "Stop."

"No, I don't think I will." He rose up on his elbow and continued to trail his hand everywhere while staring at her sweet face, which he now knew hid a very adventurous woman.

Her eyes misted, and for long minutes, they stared at one another like two teenagers gawking, as if they'd discovered sex. As if nothing in the world existed but the other person.

Her hand then drifted down his chest to grasp his cock. He knew nothing about this woman, did he? She was no saint. She was better.

He pressed her back into the mattress and took her again —this time for longer, until his name rose from her throat, filling his ears.

26

Hank Carter leaned back in his chair. "Thanks for coming in on a Sunday."

Dan Plunkett, a partner he rarely encountered, sat perched on the edge of his desk, stretching a rubber band between his hands. "Haven't seen you as much on weekends."

"No. Work-life balance and all that." Nick scrubbed his hair. He hadn't expected their text that morning. Of course, he hadn't expected to wake up to one voluptuous pie queen, either. He'd had little time to say goodbye to her after their night of finding out even more about Chloe's sensual side.

"You've had quite a few wins lately. I'd say the time off is doing you some good." Hank thunked his chair to upright and rose. "Which is why we're here to talk about moving you up."

"And out. Figuratively speaking, of course. The Los Angeles office is yours. You'll be under Peter Masqual's management tutelage for a while, but you'll get the hang of it soon enough. Then, we'd like to see a thirty percent expansion on the client side once you're through the hiring, taking over a few of our West Coast clients and…"

The words ceased to have meaning. Then again, he only half-listened after hearing the one word he'd been begging for—*yours*. Finally. All the weekends, all the sleepless nights, all the years he'd toed the line finally had paid off.

Dan held out his hand. 'So, can we count on you?"

More than. He took the handshake offer. "One thousand percent."

Hank nodded once. "Good. Contract amendment will be on your desk first thing Monday. So, now. Go. Have the rest of your weekend."

His weekend? Shit, he was going to have to break it to Chloe carefully. He could explain this development. People did long-distance relationships all the time—a term he'd never thought he'd entertain. He wasn't letting her go. He certainly wouldn't see her with Russell again—ever. Maybe she'd move with him.

His sister would love Chloe.

He ran his hand down his face as he strode to his office. Getting ahead of himself, as usual, he chided his overactive imagination.

They'd figure something out.

Around the corner, his gaze caught Mark Carter hovering nearby. No doubt trying to eavesdrop.

"Nick," he lifted his chin toward him.

He nodded once and ducked into the kitchen. He needed coffee like he needed oxygen.

Mark naturally followed him in. "So, heard you're making partner."

"Yes." He yanked open the cabinet door to retrieve a coffee filter.

"Your girlfriend going to make the move with you? To L.A., I mean."

That got his attention. Mark was fishing—and Nick needed to cut his line.

Balancing her two pies, Chloe pushed her car door shut with her foot. Nick had left early for an office meeting, and she'd had to do something with all her pent-up energy.

She'd had enough pecans to make Nick's favorite, and she decided at the last minute to bake a sugar cream pie with all the leftover brown sugar. That stuff turned to concrete in an instant once the box was open.

Her thighs complained as she took the stairs leading up to the front door, praying someone was behind the front desk and would let her in so she wouldn't have to call him. She'd wanted to surprise him—then, maybe they could have a second go at *shenanigans* in his office.

That man brought out all kinds of things in her—and she wasn't sorry for it.

The guard held the door open. "Miss Hart."

"Oh, you remembered me."

"How could I forget?" He eyed her pie.

"You like sugar cream pie?"

The man rocked back on his heels. "They call that Hoosier pie where I'm from. My late wife used to make them every Sunday."

She held it out to him. "Your lucky day then." She'd spread the luck around. She lowered her voice. "Make a wish when you eat it."

He chuckled and took her offering. "Thank you. I'll do that. Nick's upstairs. I'll buzz him."

"Oh, can we make it a surprise? I won't tell anyone you let me go up unannounced. And I promise there is no razor saw in this pecan..." she lifted it up to his face, "to bust him out of the office."

He gave her a wide smile. "It'll be our secret."

She winked at him—and for once didn't feel like an idiot when she did it. Nick and his influences.

The elevator moved at the pace of pastry dough rising, and her belly danced with anticipation at finding Nick in his office. She was a tad chafed between her legs, but maybe he'd be willing to let her return a certain favor she owed him. His mouth had gone to town on her in his office, and she could do the same—even if she'd risk industrial carpet burns on her knees. Maybe he'd eat some pie while she sampled him.

She giggled at the image of *that one*.

The doors cracked open, and the familiar office carpet smell rose up. Muffled male voices were someplace in the distance. She didn't find Nick in his office but heard his voice from somewhere. Maybe the kitchen?

As she grew closer, it was most definitely him, talking to another guy who sounded familiar, but she couldn't place him.

"You're being cagey. So, how *is* Chloe?" the unseen voice asked.

"Beats me." Nick's voice was flat.

"I thought you two were a thing. But if not, free market and all. I'll—"

"Nah. She's crazy." A muffled slap, like someone clapped another on the back sounded. "Stick with your blond. Trust me on this one."

A sick twist in her belly made her hunch a little. She had to work to take in a breath.

She peeked around the door's edge to find Nick and Mark—she thought that was his name—huddling over the coffee maker.

Two buddies hanging around, talking trash… about her. There had to be a reason for this sudden turn. Nick hadn't lied to her last night. When he held her, made love to her, couldn't seem to stop touching her—all of it felt too good.

Mark spoke again. "So, the L.A. office. Lucky dude. All those hot wannabe models trying to be actresses."

"You got that right." The clank of the coffee filter being put back in its place had her jerk herself backward. She didn't want to be seen.

"Does this mean I can have your office?" Mark chuckled. "I mean, since you get the chicks."

"Don't get ahead of yourself, Carter. But, yeah, whatever. I won't need it. I'm not coming back to this tiny town. Nothing here for me."

Nothing.

Her muscles seized as if her skin was shrinking around them.

He'd got the job he wanted. Got his partners to see him how they wanted. And she'd helped make that happen. That was the deal, right? He *won*—the position, the office, and...

He'd warned her. *Men want to win.* He'd won, alright—not only in his office but in her bedroom.

Her jaw became unhinged, and she couldn't seem to close her own mouth. He not only got everything he wanted, but as an added bonus, he also got to pull one over on Russell.

Finally, her mouth closed when something snapped inside her. Suzette Marie could have all the men. Chloe was done with these games.

She'd truly believed he was the better man. It turned out he was just better at competing. He had one thing right. She was a prize—and one he no longer had use for.

Well, too bad. She wasn't available anyway.

She backtracked to the elevators but then changed her mind. She scooted to his office and set the pie down. Three boxes stood neatly stacked in the corner, ready to haul Nick Hollister right out of Moorsville. She easily found a piece of paper and pen because the man's desk was littered with work stuff.

Good luck in L.A. I'm sure you'll be very successful because you're good at winning, just like you told me all men want to be. Lesson learned.

He brought a lot of things out in her, alright—one of them being the fool.

27

Nick paced and rubbed his scalp nearly raw from scrubbing his nails through it. "Chloe, I came by your apartment, but you must be out. I've got to explain a few things... about L.A." It was similar to the message he'd left an hour ago, which wasn't returned.

He fingered her note. Chloe was pissed. The only logical thing that came to mind was she'd overheard him and Mark. Or, perhaps she ran into Hank or Dan on the way out, and they spilled the proverbial beans. Either way, she had an idea in her head that he needed to set straight.

"Listen, I don't know if you're really pissed or if this is a misunderstanding, but... call me back, okay?"

He shoved his phone into his jeans pocket and yanked open the front door of Peppermint Sweet. A familiar face beamed at him from behind the glass counter.

"Hey, Scarlett." He slapped both hands on the edge of the counter.

She smiled. "Hello there, handsome."

"You talk to Chloe today?" Women talked to each other about everything.

It Was All The Pie's Fault

"Uh-uh." She squinched her eyes and cocked her head. "You two have a fight or something? You got that look in your eye."

Why men were not terrified of female intuition, he'd never know. They saw too much—and Chloe had definitely heard or seen something she was interpreting wrong.

He straightened and shrugged. "When you do, tell her I'm sorry and I can explain."

She crossed her arms over her chest. "What did you do?" Jesus, women adopted the mom voice quickly. He didn't know if Scarlett had any children, but he suddenly felt twelve years old again and had gotten caught sneaking cookies.

His hand found its way to his hair again and he raked his fingers through. "Nothing. Tell her we won, and emphasize the *we* part."

Scarlett's forehead bunched. "Um, man code? Explain, please."

"She'll know what I mean."

"You can't tell her this because…" She flipped her hand over and curled her fingers in a tell-me-more gesture.

"She's not answering her phone."

Scarlett's chin raised high. "Oooh. You *are* in trouble." She fanned both her hands. "Okay, I'll give her a message, but don't expect miracles. Not unless you're on your knees and bestowing gifts." She pointed her finger at him. "Remember my wisdom, grasshopper."

He huffed and spun himself out of there. Chloe had to answer him eventually, right?

Jesus, he was cooked with this woman. Any other female who conveniently had misunderstood something and didn't return his messages to at least clarify things would be off his radar screen in a nanosecond.

He pulled out his phone to check if she'd responded. Nada.

She'd call him. She would.

Except she didn't on Sunday, and stalking her apartment felt untenable even to him. Hadn't he been the one to warn her of stalking?

Yeah, that promise lasted until Sunday night. He knocked on her door and either she didn't answer or wasn't home. But to not be home the night before a Monday when she had to be at school?

Jesus, if something had happened to her… He had to wait twenty-four hours before filing a missing person's report. And what would he say? She's not answering my sort-of apology? She might have dumped my ass?

He went home and ate her fantastic pecan pie she'd left—and even scattered a few wishes into the Universe. This state he found himself in? It was ridiculous.

He could wait her out. He didn't need to leave for L.A. for another ten days—as if he'd wait that long. Maybe this was a sign for him to move to the West Coast early.

Signs, wishes. Man, he was going off the deep end.

He waited until Monday afternoon to show up at her school—and only because he found his number blocked when he tried her line for the hundredth time. She wasn't just angry, she was done. So what? He was going to say his piece if nothing else.

As he strode across the polished school floor in the expansive and too-quiet hallway, he had half a mind to jet straight to her classroom. But respect shown was respect earned, so he stopped at the front office.

A lone woman stood behind the desk, stapling some papers. She peered over her glasses at him. "Can I help you?"

"I'm here to see Chloe Hart." He tried to look non-menacing, whatever that meant.

"Are you a parent?"

He shook his head. "A friend."

It Was All The Pie's Fault

"It's spring break this week. All the teachers and students are off. Can I leave a message?"

He tugged on his hair—again. This was not how things were supposed to go.

But maybe they were. He had a new office across the country to lead, and one weekend wasn't enough to change that plan. Maybe he should let her go. She'd be more wary of men next time, which wasn't a bad thing. Then again, she might revert to her old ways of basically doing what he was doing right now—stalking a romantic interest.

Jesus, romance. Nothing should be further from his mind right now.

He turned to head out but his gaze caught a bright pink sheet of paper tacked to a large corkboard. It was a flyer for a kid's show next weekend—the night he'd catch the red-eye out of here.

Chloe's face beamed from a picture. She wore a huge men's shirt splashed with blue and yellow paint. She was smiling down at two little boys who held their paintbrushes high as if waving a sword. Fuck, she was hot.

Okay, he was officially losing his ever-loving mind.

He drew closer to the picture. His stupid heart tugged a little at seeing her smile. Chloe Hart really was beautiful—both inside and out.

Which meant what? He hadn't a clue how to do any of this wanting-a-woman stuff. How to be with a woman who believed her pies were magic, who couldn't bring herself to say *fuck*, who wore a cherry print skirt. Well, that last one was smokin'.

In the end, however, letting her go would be wise for both him and her.

He untacked the flyer and turned to the front desk woman. "Mind if I take this?"

If nothing else, it could be a souvenir.

28

Chloe twiddled with the spoon in her coffee cup and yawned. She should have slept better in that little cabin in the woods.

It was a spot no one had wanted because it had no air conditioning, television, or wireless Internet, so she'd easily booked it at the last minute. The isolation was supposed to help clear her head. Nothing like listening to the birds in the morning and wind through the pine trees to give one over to their thoughts.

Only, she hated what her mind conjured right now. She'd been played—maybe.

A little time in the woods and doubts began to creep inside. She refused to believe Nick was truly *so* heartless he'd be warning other guys off her, calling her crazy. Not the Nick she knew.

But did she really know him? Hardly. And his voice that day in his office sounded so sure.

She's crazy.

Hot wannabe models.

Nothing here for me.

That last one really hurt. They'd *had* something. Not nothing.

His first message after receiving her note was a little accusatory. Like he could tell she'd overheard something and she'd been actually crazy to believe what her own ears took in. His second message was the typical "I can explain" excuse. Yeah, they usually could.

So, when she returned—to lay aside any lingering doubts—she'd made one last-ditch effort to clarify things. She'd texted him this morning after unblocking him. Yeah, she'd been that childish.

Her message was simple, direct.

<<I'm listening.>>

It took him less than thirty seconds to answer her.

<<Now? Enjoy Russell.>>

Oh, *he* was angry at *her*. That was rich. *Whatever.* Her fingers hovered over her phone. "Go ahead and move to L.A. and bang all the hot models you can find," is what she wanted to text back.

Instead, she toyed with blocking him again but chose not to for reasons she couldn't have said if someone threatened to bash her with a rolling pin.

"Enjoy Russell," she said to her tea. "Yeah, right." Another woman could do that. She felt nothing for Russell Montgomery Langston, the man who was *not* going to father her children. Her ovaries were off-limits to the player.

The fact that Nick had been right galled her. But she was glad to know who Russell really was.

She lifted the tinfoil on the pie she'd made that morning —a cherry for the hell of it. It would be a reminder, a talisman to not throw her love wishes in the wrong direction. Nana had been right, as usual. Why had she forgotten her warning until now?

She'd give anything to have her Nana here right now. She'd know what to do next.

An idea thunked into her brain. She gazed up at the ceiling. "Thanks, Nana." The solution was so simple. Today, she'd wish for anyone who ate it to find their true love—emphasis on *true*. She'd ask for nothing in return. Maybe then, the Universe, God, or whatever was working things would make it right.

Suzette Marie's light laughter filled the room. Her arm was hooked in Bradley's, and he beamed down at her as they strode into the staff lounge. First, they both looked entirely too awake for 7 a.m. on a Monday, and two, wow, does she work fast in the man department.

"'Allo." Suzette Marie kissed Chloe on the cheek.

"How was Paris?" Gah, she sounded like a cheerleader on speed, all high-pitched and jumpy—not that she knew what taking speed felt like.

"It was wonderful to be home, but I missed everyone here." She glanced over at Bradley, who flushed.

He slipped his arm free. "I've got to get going. The ruffians are about to descend." He waved at Chloe and turned away.

"Bradley looks smitten." Like a kitten—totally oblivious to the cruelty of the love world.

Suzette Marie waved her hand. "He is sweet."

Chloe rose. She should get to her classroom and organize art supplies or something before the masses descended. "There's pie if you'd like it." She wafted her hand over the thing. Then Nana's words rang out. *Everyone has to benefit when you use the pies.*

Chloe paused and traced her finger on a crack of the wooden table. "About Russell. In case he didn't tell you, he tried to kiss me while you were gone. He's bad news. I mean, in case he continues to go after you." The sisterhood required

It Was All The Pie's Fault

she at least be honest with Suzette Marie, in case she deigned to eat of Chloe's pie.

Suzette Marie appeared quite puzzled. "What about Nick?"

"Oh." She flapped her hand. "We're not a thing anymore."

"That's good?" Suzette Marie asked.

"Yes. We both deserve better men. Like you said."

"Ah, Nick. Not so... deserving?"

Chloe pulled out a chair, the scrape of the metal chair making them both wince, and plunked herself down. A fatigue had settled in her legs. "Nick just wanted to win me. Like Russell did you."

Suzette Marie tsked. "Men. Such beasts."

"You got that right. Hey, you want some pie?" She pushed the pie toward Suzette Marie. "It's magic. Make a wish and it'll come true. Wish for someone more deserving. Like Bradley maybe?"

Suzette Marie sat down in the chair next to her. "Maybe. But I think I will—and make this wish you say." She stared at the pie, not taking a piece. She lifted her blue eyes to her. "If I did have a wish, it would be to be close friends. With you."

Now Chloe was speechless. First, she'd *consider* eating sugar, and second, friends?

She waved her hand, her gold bracelets dangling. "I envy you, Chloe. I don't make friends easily."

Chloe blinked at her. She'd not really given Suzette Marie a chance, and in a way, the men in their lives had played them both. She'd rather hang out with women right now anyway. She could so totally get why women formed communes and why the all-woman Themyscira was first called Paradise Island.

She clasped Suzette Marie's hand. "We're already friends. Who else is going to show me the best manicure place in town?" She'd never entertained doing that before so she honestly didn't know.

"It's Elodie's. Market Street." She half-smiled. "I was holding out on you. But..." she squared herself to Chloe, "not anymore. Saturday? Or are you baking?"

"I'm going to take a break from that. I mean, I'll always make pies, but maybe it's time to do more."

"Good. Because you're really talented with pastry."

"And maybe you can teach me to swear in French." That wouldn't be breaking her oath to herself, would it? And it was time to break out a little.

Suzette Marie's face inched up into her seductive smile. "With pleasure."

29

Nick put the phone on speaker and picked up the boxing tape. "Daph, you'll love L.A. Sunshine year round. Good schools."

His sister sighed on the other end of the phone. "It's not… us."

What the hell did that mean? "You prefer year-round rain? Because that's all it seems to do around here." He ripped off a long piece and placed it over the last box that was headed to L.A. later that afternoon.

"April showers bring May flowers."

Now it was his time to huff out a sigh. "Come on. Just consider it." Her deadbeat ex may be leaving her alone right now, but he didn't trust the guy long-term.

"What does your girlfriend think of year-round sunshine?"

"I don't have a girlfriend."

"Nick." Jesus, the mom voice was *right there*. It had to be part of female genes. "What did you do?"

Why did everyone conclude automatically it was him? "Nothing."

He stared down at the box he'd just taped up. He couldn't recall what was inside in order to label it. He truly was losing his mind.

Daphne laughed a little. "Uh-huh. Go back to packing. We'll talk later. The little man is getting antsy. We're going outside—in the *rain*." She sobered. "But, Nick, I find the truth usually works pretty well."

"Truthfully, I want you and Benjamin to come with me."

She scoffed into the earpiece. "No, Nicholas. With your mystery girlfriend."

His sister was the only person on the planet who'd call him by his full name. "Not happening. I'll call you later so I can continue to convince you to move."

"You can try, but..." Daphne's voice said something to someone in the distance. "Listen, Nick, I have to go. Let me know you arrived, okay?"

"I will. And please reconsider."

"I won't. L.A. isn't our kind of town. I love you."

After they killed the call, he positioned the box cutter to slice through the tape. For the last few nights, he'd been throwing things in boxes, yanking clothes off clothes hangers. He didn't have time to do anything but multi-task.

He'd been trying to tie up loose ends after days of endless calls, meetings, and texts to begin his new life as head of WSC's Southern California office—and all of that on top of his regular client base.

His clients weren't happy he was leaving. They seemed to be the only ones.

Other associates jockeyed for his office. His landlord had six people wanting this apartment. The only person who appeared fine with him turning left and headed out west was Chloe. Not his girlfriend. Not his anything.

She'd unblocked him, but that didn't mean she answered his texts like a grown-ass adult. So, he'd gotten a little snarky back at her. So what? She'd left him churning, stewing. Nick didn't *stew*—not over women.

The box cutter slipped and cut the cardboard down the side. Shit—thinking of that woman made him lose his faculties.

He rose and threw the thing across the room. Not his finest moment, especially when it was open and cut a long slice in the drywall when it hit. He kicked the box of books in front of him as if that would solve a damned thing.

Chloe was killing him. His sister and nephew were, too. The only thing he could get her to promise involved this stupid little town.

Daph said she could move to Moorsville—something about it being "more her vibe"—and that he should jet off to the west by himself. "Take stock of what you really wanted by trying it out before committing," she'd said.

He knew what he wanted. Except, the closer he grew to flight day, doubts had crept in like ants at a picnic. Like he'd ever had time for going on a picnic.

He'd throw another box cutter if he had one. He didn't have time for indecision. He upended the box. Papers and picture frames spilled out.

A bright pink piece of paper stood out. He didn't even need to unfurl its edges to know what it was.

Spring Fling at Moorsville Elementary School
All grades. All Fun.

Shit, the show was tonight. Daphne was right. Maybe it was time to throw some truth out there—starting with saying his piece to a certain woman who believed in magic pies. He had to rid himself of his obsessive thoughts about Chloe—leave them all behind in Moorsville. Because he was getting on that damned airplane.

30

Screaming, high-pitched voices of little kids and the din of stressed and proud parents mixed together filled the parking lot as people streamed up the steps to go into the school.

He was worse off than he thought. Weeks ago, he'd have never known how to navigate an elementary school parking lot. Now, he strode across the asphalt to the back entrance with ease.

He yanked open the door, yellow light spilling out onto the landing.

The main hall was lined with tables draped in paper tablecloths. Bowls of chips and plates of cookies and other dishes covered every inch of the surface. His heart skipped a ridiculous beat at seeing pies among them.

He walked up to a table where a woman sporting a clown costume sat, ripping little red tickets off a huge roll. She smiled up at him—the greasepaint creating a macabre grin. "Here for the show?"

He tamped down the snarky remark sitting on his tongue. *No, I'm here to sneak a cookie. And rid myself of obsessing over one pie queen.* "Yes. I'll take one ticket."

It Was All The Pie's Fault

She handed him one. "I don't recognize you. You have a student here?"

"I'm with Chloe Hart." Saying the words did something inside him. Figuring out what that something actually represented, however, was lost on him.

"Oh? She didn't mention anything." But her painted face stretched into a creepy smile again. "Enjoy the show."

He nodded and spun away.

It wasn't hard to find Chloe. He rounded the corner towards the noise and nearly ran her over.

Her hand slapped her chest. "*Merde alors.* Nick."

His arms shot out, and his hands curled around her biceps. Jesus, she felt good. Warm. His breath instantly caught. "I knew you could say the F word."

She freed herself and crossed her arms. "It actually means the…" she lowered her voice, "*poop* word. Besides, it's French, so it doesn't count."

"Oh, it counts. And it means both." Her arms stayed banded over her. Still trying to hide herself. Well, he'd found her.

His heart ratcheted up at seeing she wore her cherry print skirt and the white sweater she swore she never wore.

"Wandering around an elementary school again? The show is for the students and paying guests." Her Miss Prim voice was on full blast. Did she have any idea what an effect that had on him?

He held up his ticket stub. "Paying guest."

She sighed heavily. "Why are you here?"

"I needed to see you before—"

"Before you jet off to your supermodel coast? Good luck." She tried to scoot by him, but he stopped her.

"Thanks. But before I leave, I want to know what happened. Between us. Mystery and I don't match." So much for the little speech he was going to give. The one filled with "good luck", "good riddance", and "we're no longer a fit". Not when she stood there appearing so defiant and adorable.

Her lips thinned. "I left you a note at your office. You do read, right? Or shall I have one of my first graders interpret for you?"

A chuckle escaped his throat, but he sobered quickly. "And then you blocked my return messages."

She sniffed. "I unblocked you."

"Eventually. But you didn't answer me then, either."

"I was mad," she shouted and immediately stepped backward as if shocked by herself.

Something batted his knees. Peering down, he caught a giant pink wing bobbing up and down as the little girl who'd smacked him with her fairy costume jogged by. She gasped, turned, and her eyes widened. Man, those little ones sneak right up on you.

Chloe peered down at her. "Not at you, Bethany. You're beautiful and wonderful."

The little girl's face broke into a big smile, then her big brown eyes gazed up at Nick. "What did you do?"

Jesus. Did every female in the world think he was Satan?

Chloe grasped the little girl's hand. "Told you six-year-olds miss nothing."

Okay, ganged up on by a woman in a cherry print skirt—and yes it was still hot—and a girl in a fairy costume.

Chloe cleared her throat. "The thing is, Mr. Hollister." Her voice was calm—too calm. Things were bad, weren't they? "I understand all your lessons now. Like you said. Certain... *people* in the world just want to win, and you did. You got all you wanted. There's nothing more to say."

His brain flooded with things to say to her. But words—his stock in trade—failed him. Seeing her, being this close to her and that damnable cherry print skirt, caused a mind-blanking lust to rise up. He was a man, after all.

No, she was more than an object of desire to him. His shoulders unknotted for the first time in a week, and his gut lurched anew with a new realization.

He couldn't stand being away from this woman. Nothing about his life fit without her.

"There's plenty left to say. I want you." Rule number one of negotiation. Don't say you want something unless you're willing to lose it. So why in the ever-loving world did those three words come out of his mouth?

Maybe because he meant it.

He did. God help him, he wanted Chloe.

He closed the distance between them. In his periphery, he could see the little girl's gaze dart back and forth between them.

His mouth was too dry. "And you got... who you wanted. Russell." He was fishing. But even if Nick and Chloe had slept together, she now had options. The wholly-undeserving guy had obviously noticed her—thanks to their charade.

"I don't want him." Her chin lifted. "I deserve better." She peered down at Bethany. "Remember, no frogs, only princes."

The little girl nodded vigorously and then looked at Nick. "Which one are you?"

Oh, God. He was the frog, wasn't he? "I'm trying to be the prince." He moved his gaze back to Chloe. "Whatever I did that put me in the amphibian category..." He'd crossed into some third dimension with this kind of talk. "Whatever it is you think I did, I'm sorry."

Chloe stilled, then knelt down before Bethany. "Can you run and find Meredith? Check her wings for me?"

"Oh, yes." With a job assigned, the little girl was gone in a flash.

Chloe rose slowly and smoothed down her skirt. "You called me crazy." She moved to turn away, but he grasped her arm.

"Well…" He tried to put on a smile. "You do believe in magic pies."

She whirled on him. "They are!" She yanked free and stomped off.

He just could not get himself off a lily pad, could he? He easily caught up to her and made her face him. "No, Chloe. Did it ever occur to you that it's you? *You're* the magic."

"I am not."

"You believe in your pies more than you? You're the one who makes everything better. You made my life better. It's not pastry and…" and he waved his hand, "fluff and stuff that makes things happen."

A giggle erupted from her throat.

"Why are you laughing?"

"You said fluff and stuff. Is that an official legal term?"

The relief at hearing the ease in her voice coursed through his body was like a drug. The remaining knots in his shoulder loosened. "You have no idea how much of an official legal term that is."

Her frown returned. "Why did you tell Mark I was crazy?"

Oh. Suddenly, everything made sense. She truly *had* overheard everything he'd said that day to ward off the fucker,

"That was to keep him away from you. He's Russell times one hundred. All he'd want is to get into your oven."

She scoffed. "Why bother caring who is in my oven? You're leaving. There's nothing here for you—your words exactly."

"There's plenty here for me."

"My pies? My magic?"

He had to give her credit. She was committed to her voodoo. "They aren't—"

"They *are*."

"*You're* magic. More than anyone deserves."

It Was All The Pie's Fault

She blinked at him. "Oh." Her face grew steely again. "Yes, I am and you blew it," she huffed out fiercely.

"Did I?" She'd overheard lies and believed them. He wouldn't be sorry for keeping the wolves off her. "Did it ever occur to you I was trying to protect you? That I found you special enough to only want you to have what *you* want?"

She blinked up at him. "What do you mean?"

"Chloe, I still don't believe your pies are magic. But I know one thing—I love you, and I'm not going to stand around and watch men like Russell and Mark and... what?" She was staring at him as if he'd slapped her. Hell, he'd take a man's arm off if anyone did that to her.

"You... you love me?"

"Yes." A few heads turned on his half-shout. Enough words. He grasped her arms and brought his lips as close to hers as he dared. "I really do."

She trembled under his hands, but then her lips met his, and any thought of propriety went out the front door. The woman's kissing ability needed to be trademarked, one that only he was allowed to indulge in. He was an attorney. He could do it.

Little girl voices squealed all around them mixed with a little boy's voice making a retching sound. Nick still couldn't stop moving his mouth over hers.

Chloe broke the kiss and panted a little. "We're in front of everyone."

"Good. Witnesses define and enlighten the truth."

A tall man with his arms crossed behind Chloe cleared his throat.

She glanced at him and stepped backward. "Oh. Sorry. Nick, this is Mr. Markinson, the principal."

He arched an eyebrow at Nick.

Nick raised both hands. "Sorry, Principal. I'm proposing here. I'm going to marry Chloe."

Chloe's eyes flew wide. She took two steps backward. "You're... what?"

"Show us the ring! Show us the ring!" The little fairy was back, her wings bobbing as she jumped around like a jackrabbit.

But she had a point. He once more closed the gap between them. "You were right, Miss Hart. They miss nothing." He glanced down at the circle of little girls who'd appeared out of nowhere like little ninjas. "Okay, then how about I let Miss Hart pick it out herself?"

The little fairy frowned. "Nooo. You have to get on one knee and present it."

"And wear a suit. A *good* one." A little girl in a unicorn onesie nodded.

Nick tsked. "Schooled by a six-year-old."

"They're smart." Chloe's voice was soft, a sheen of wet shone in her eyes.

"Okay, then. I know this little place with the best coffee and pies and chairs with hearts scrolled on them. We're doing it there." He moved to kiss her again—hang the principal—but her hands slapped his pecs.

She peered up at him. "I'm not moving to Los Angeles."

"Then neither am I." He almost couldn't believe those words escaped his mouth, but they felt... *right*.

"Can you do that?"

"Sure. I know this girl. She can make wishes come true so all I have to do is—"

"Believe."

"Eh. There may be some negotiating that has to be engaged..." More like groveling. He couldn't cross that magic belief line completely.

"You're pretty good at that." She flushed. "And other things."

He took both her hands. God, he loved this pie queen and

It Was All The Pie's Fault

her dirty mind, "I still need to do some proving of those other things, however. After the show."

"You're staying?" She raised an eyebrow. "I mean, really?"

"I can't leave the best pie I've ever tasted. I saw them out there."

She slapped his pec once more and quickly glanced down at the knot of little women and then back up at him. "There *are* more flavors to try."

"I'm counting on it."

She smiled, and Los Angeles was suddenly some overpriced real estate with silicone-injected women that he'd be glad to miss.

Huh. Maybe Chloe's spell on him would wear off someday. Today was not that day.

"No," she said.

What? He'd missed something. And it was important. "You're turning me down?"

"No, but Los Angeles is your dream. You have to at least give the West Coast a try."

"But—"

"I mean it. Otherwise, you'll always wonder. I'm pretty stubborn."

"You don't say." He had to admit, a wash of relief moved over him. He'd worked damned hard for the L.A. promotion. "Long-distance can work."

"I want a first-class ticket both ways when you invite me."

He chuffed. "Suzette Marie is rubbing off on you."

"She's a great friend. Learning all kinds of things. Like letting people choose for themselves. Not relying so much on…" She glanced down at her feet.

He tipped her chin up with one finger. "Please don't tell me you're going to stop baking."

Her chin jutted backward. "Never. I mean, it brought you to me. I think my wish did come true."

This woman would never quit with the magic stuff, would she? He was okay with it, actually. "You're one of a kind, Chloe. I'll give you that."

Her eyes misted. "I am."

Screw the fact that they stood in an elementary school. He kissed her again. Her lips tasted like cherry pie. Maybe their meeting over a baked good was kismet. Maybe she'd hypnotized him. Who cared? He had his arms full of his woman—the *right* woman.

EPILOGUE

The bell over Peppermint Sweet's front door tinkled its welcome song as she entered. Such a happy sound. Such a happy place.

Out of habit, Chloe glanced over at the little bistro table with the heart chairs in the front window. Two women were sitting there, their heads bowed and talking excitedly. Ah, well, she told Nick she'd grab the spot if it was available.

Scarlett rushed over to her and grabbed the top two boxes from her armful. "Do you ever stop glowing? No, wait, don't tell me. Nick did his magic thing to you."

She bumped her hip against Scarlett's "Get your mind out of the gutter. It's not magic. It's... *beyond* magic." She winked at her friend—something her eyes couldn't stop doing all the time now.

"So, give me some good news." Scarlett hoofed it to the countertop with her other pies. "I need it."

"Bad first date?"

"The. Worst. He was good with his hands, though."

"You didn't." Chloe set her bag down at her feet.

"What? A girl has needs. Besides, he needed to stop

talking so I gave him something else to do with that mouth. And unlike you, I don't have a hunky attorney at my beck and call every day."

"He's not at my beck and call."

Scarlett eyed her.

"Okay. But only some days." Chloe smiled. Like the days he was in town. He'd moved to Los Angeles almost immediately after the kids' show and had been gone for an interminable two weeks, only coming back last Friday for one quick weekend before he had to catch the red-eye tonight.

Her resolve that a long-distance relationship could work? Waning by the second.

Still, she let that wish he would bag Los Angeles, move back to Moorsville, and finally freaking propose already sit on her tongue unspoken. She'd learned her lesson about pushing the magic luck too far. She also liked the idea he'd ask her on her own, making his own decisions around her.

At least, she would for another few days. She wasn't a saint.

The last few weeks had been terrible without him. She wasn't sure she could stand it much longer, and they'd just gotten started.

They Facetimed for hours every night, but it wasn't the same—not even when she discovered the joys—and necessity —of phone sex. It was most definitely *not the same* as having him in her bed. Or helping her with baking like he had earlier this morning—in the nude. That was super-fun.

For now, she had to be conscious to tamp down the resentment he'd been called into the office on their last day together for yet another two weeks.

Scarlett peered toward the door. "Where is your hot, sugar-addicted hottie anyway?"

"He dropped me off. He had to go by his office. His partners called him in for yet another emergency something-or-other." Their sudden need to meet him on a Sunday didn't compute with their adamant work balance ideas.

She pulled out the last pie from its box. "Dang it."

"What's wrong?"

"I sent Nick off with the pineapple pie instead of the chocolate." Mr. Carter had asked—if it wasn't too much trouble—if Chloe could send another pie along sometime. With pleasure. Maybe it'd help get him out early today.

Scarlett scoffed. "It doesn't matter what kind of pie. They'll love it. Pineapple signifies luck and prosperity, right?"

"It does. But still..." Her lips puffed out in a pout. Maybe Suzette Marie was rubbing off on her as much as Nick was. Winking. Pouting. Her face did so many things now that it hadn't before.

Scarlett licked her thumb as some chocolate had conveniently gotten on it when she lifted out the chocolate creme pie. "Want some tea?"

"I'd love that. I've got time." Her phone buzzed. She glanced down and, seeing who it was, sighed. She lifted her phone and tapped out a message. "I'll be late for a meeting with Russell, but whatever."

Scarlett's eyes widened, and Chloe raised her hand in a stop sign motion. "Since Nick had to go to work I agreed to help out Russell. Don't worry. Nick knows." Russell was working every angle to get to spend time with her. As if anything he could do would woo her away from Nick.

A man's voice boomed near the doorway. "They say this place is amazing."

She turned to watch a tall, lanky guy enter with a pretty brunette. She said something that Chloe couldn't catch. It wasn't lost on her that they immediately approached the little bistro table with the heart-shaped chairs, now empty of the two women. The woman flushed from eyelashes to ankles when the man pulled out her chair for her.

They were most definitely on a date.

More people streamed into the shop, and Chloe hung around the counter, not wanting to take up any of the tables and chairs with her slow sipping of her tea. She amused herself by watching the couple.

The man got two coffees for himself and the woman and then hovered near the glassed baked goods display. He swiped his hair back and glanced over at the woman then back at the case.

"Can I get you anything?" Scarlett asked him.

"Trying to decide what she might like. Maybe I should go ask, huh?" He gave her a sheepish smile. So nervous. So adorable.

Chloe sidled up to him. "I recommend the cherry," she whispered. "And make a wish when she eats it." She glanced over to the woman sitting nervously by the window. She checked her manicure, smoothed down her top. Oh, she was into this guy.

The man blinked at her like she was crazy.

"For love." She glanced once more at the woman who was now fussing with her hair. She was into him, alright. Chloe knew all the signals now—both from men and women now that she'd gone through Nick's school of men.

He swallowed and nodded. "Couldn't hurt, I guess."

"Not at all."

As soon as he was gone, she called Scarlett over. "Make *sure* they have the cherry."

Scarlett glanced at the man and then back at her. "On it."

Chloe then took her time sipping her tea, enjoying a few moments to herself. She tried not to stare too hard at the couple as they shared a piece of her cherry pie. When the man slid a forkful of the pie into her mouth, Chloe then sent the mantra through the ethers.

. . .

It Was All The Pie's Fault

To all who eat
   This salt and sweet
   I bless your wish
   With my dish.
   If good and true
   It comes to you.
   Embrace the light
   And take a bite.

She glanced at the woman sitting in her chair. Her eyes glowed, and she leaned forward toward the man. Yes, Nana would approve if she made a wish for them.

I wish for that couple to find true love today.

The man then stood and held out his arm to the woman. Oh, that was fast. Now, if only Nick moved that fast.

Maybe the magic was on fire today. *I wish for the best outcome with Nick, too,* she thought quickly. With any luck, he'd had some of the pineapple she'd sent, and it couldn't hurt to make a generic wish. It wasn't too specific so it wasn't exactly going against her self-oath to have patience around their relationship status.

The bell over the door tinkled again as the couple opened the door and revealed Nick about to enter. After they left, he moved inside, his face beaming a huge smile at seeing her.

She met him halfway and he lifted her off her feet into a bear hug.

"Whoa, someone's in a good mood."

"I am. Got my arms full of my pie queen." He set her back on her feet. "Plus, I've got news." He glanced back at the bistro table, now abandoned by the couple, except a man hovered nearby, dropping his sweatshirt on the back of one of the chairs.

"Hold up." Nick grew so serious. He strode over to the guy.

"Hey, man, do me a favor? I need this table. My girlfriend likes it. It's the hearts on the chairs."

The man arched his eyebrow, glanced over at her, then chuckled. "Man, someone's whipped."

"You have no idea."

Her heart flipped a little at hearing his words.

The man grabbed his sweatshirt. "Table's yours." With a smirk, he strode away.

Nick dropped his suit coat over the back of the chair as if marking his territory.

"What was that?" Chloe asked when he returned to her.

"It's our place." He set his hand on her back, steering her to the table. Flutters started in her lower belly that he did that for her.

He scrubbed his jaw. "Like I said, I've got news." His happy smile was replaced with nerves that seemed to dance under his skin.

She sat down and put her purse by her feet. "It doesn't look like very good news." Now her heart was thumping like a tribal chant.

He took the chair opposite her, resting both his arms across the table, palms up.

"How bad is it?" She set her hands in his. "Your meeting? What happened?"

"It went… unexpectedly." He withdrew his arms and then moved off his chair.

"Hey, man, how are you doing?" Russell's voice boomed behind her. "Thought I'd find Chloe here when she didn't come to our meeting." He beamed at her.

"Yeah, about that. Today's not a good day after all. Let's talk Monday." She needed to find out what was up with her boyfriend, not hand-hold a man she had zero interest in.

It Was All The Pie's Fault

"But—"

"Later, man," Nick interjected. "We're in the middle of something here."

"Sure... I know you've got to catch a plane out of here soon, right?" Russell snarled.

The totally unwanted guest headed to the counter. Maybe he'd get a to-go coffee. She really had no time for Russell today. And his little dig about Nick leaving wasn't appreciated.

The bell chimes tinkled behind her again, but she had no interest to see who entered. "So, go on, you were saying?"

He fidgeted in his chair, his forehead wrinkled. "Well, first..." He looked like he was about to stand up.

"Hey, Chloe." Bradley appeared by their table with Suzette Marie hanging off his arm.

Nick let out a frustrated sigh.

Chloe smiled up at them as Suzette Marie leaned down and gave her a peck on each cheek. "We just stopped in before heading out to the park. It's such a lovely day. Time for a picnic. So good to see you here Nick. We wondered when we might see you again."

"Here I am," Nick's voice was laced was sarcasm.

Chloe's gaze shot to his. Something was definitely up. Oh, no, did something happen in L.A. that ticked off his bosses?

"Good thing, too. Our friend there..." Bradley inclined his head back to Russell, who hovered at the back counter. "has been sniffing around our girl here."

Suzette Marie's eyes widened. "Sniffing? What is this sniffing?"

"It's what a hound dog does when it's trying to get something," he laughed.

"You don't say," Nick ground out. "Listen, we'll see you later, okay?"

Bradley's smile dropped. "Sure thing, man." They turned to leave, which was good because Nick was not okay.

She grabbed his hand again. "Go on."

He swung his legs to the side. Was he adjusting his pants? He moved to get up again when Scarlett appeared.

"Last picnic basket. It's so nice out. Thought you guys might like to nab it before Bradley and Suzette do. I mean, who knew the humidity would drop so much today? Nick, I really thought you'd like it, but I guess you have to leave soon, right?"

Russell crept up behind Scarlett and peered around her. "What time did you say your flight was? Maybe we can meet after, Chloe?"

Nick threw up his hands. "People. Chloe and I are trying to have a conversation. Alone."

"Oh, right, sorry," Scarlett gave him a wide smile. "You do probably have to catch a plane soon—"

"No. I don't," he shouted. "I've been trying to tell her I'm not going back to Los Angeles."

The room grew silent. Chloe swallowed and her spine straightened. "You got fired."

He heaved out a sigh and rolled his eyes toward the ceiling. "No, I got offered equity partner here in Moorsville. If I stay. And..." he shot to standing, scraping the chair back "so everyone knows because clearly everyone is interested, my partners are worried I'm going to lose this woman, which is not going to happen because this amazing woman is mine." He pointed at her, then waved his hand. "So can everyone just back up while I get on my knees and present a diamond worthy of her. Like I promised. In this very spot."

Her whole body froze as if filled with ice. Except she wasn't cold. Her skin prickled with a strange heat. He was just so fierce with his words. Possessive. Determined.

She loved it.

It Was All The Pie's Fault

Hold the Sam Hill up. A diamond.

A slow smile spread across his face as he slunk to kneeling. He picked up her hand, reached into his trouser pocket, and pulled out a small turquoise box. Ooo, Tiffany.

He set it in the palm of her hand. "Chloe Hart..." He cracked open the box. It made a tiny squeak when he opened it. The room was silent—too silent.

She glanced up. Everyone stood around, mouths agape—except for Scarlett, who was grinning.

"I would have done this earlier, but I needed the perfect setting for us. Will you, Chloe? Marry me?"

She stared down at the two-carat heart-shaped diamond in a platinum setting. Of course, she recognized it immediately. She'd been studying it for the last nineteen days, wondering... how could he have known? He hadn't been around. Except...

She sucked in a breath. "Thanks, Nana," she whispered. Maybe her wish was granted. It wasn't that he was presenting the perfect diamond ring but that he knew her—like, truly understood her—and liked what he'd learned.

Nick arched an eyebrow. "Is that a 'yes'?"

"Yes. Yes. Yes. Yes. Yes." She slipped the ring from its cushion, but he took it from her before she could slip it on her finger.

"May I?"

She nodded.

He slipped it onto her finger and closed his hand around hers. "Thank you for making me so lucky."

The small crowd that had assembled around them burst into applause.

Nick yanked her up to standing and engulfed her in a big bear hug. "There's just one more condition. Set out by my partners."

She pulled back to look up at him. "I won't cave on the

move thing later if that's what you're going to say."

"Never. L.A.'s got too much traffic and smog anyway." He swung her a little in his arms. "And there's no Chloe pie there. Hank loved your pineapple, by the way. So, they want a pie a week. Do you think we could do that?"

She nodded. "Lots more flavors to try."

"I have to say..." he grasped her hand and stared at the ring on her finger "your pineapple today was great. And I might have thought... things when I ate it."

She gasped. "You made a wish."

"No, more like thought about how North Carolina is way cheaper than L.A., and since Daphne has agreed to move here..."

"She has?"

"Yep. So, because of that, and the fact Moorsville has only one supermodel—you—that might lure me—"

She slapped his forearm. "I don't lure."

"No. You grant wishes." And then he kissed her—in front of everyone.

She supposed, in the end, men did want to win in love. But didn't everyone?

Now, what was that final and third thing he said men wanted? Oh, to pass on their genes. And when he did, she'd teach their children how to bake. With any luck, they'd have the magic, too. Because it was real. The man standing in front of her was living proof.

Good and true.

THE END

~~~~

Thank you for reading It Was All the Pie's Fault.
If you loved Chloe and Nick's story, you'll love *It Was All The*

It Was All The Pie's Fault

Cat's Fault, the next Meet Cute series book.

~~~~~

Eve can juggle work, school and a fixer-upper house just fine with a little help from YouTube. Well, she could, if her beloved cat, Thor, would stop getting into trouble—like getting stuck behind the walls. Thankfully, plumbers make house calls at ridiculous-o'clock in the morning.

Enter Brent who not only has all the power tools she needs, he looks like the God Thor. A mountain of muscle with movie-star hair, shining green eyes, and a perfectly scruffed, chiseled jaw. *Just great.* She doesn't have time for all the lusty neediness rising where it *should not be rising*.

Eve reminds herself and her weakening knees that she's a strong, independent woman determined to make it without anyone's help. But as more renovation and cat-astrophes pile on, she finds her fingers doing the walking to call Brent to her rescue.

And she has to decide if keeping him at arm's length fits her life plan, or if it's the biggest miscalculation she's ever made.

It doesn't help Thor seems to be in cahoots with Brent when it comes to foisting romance on her.

An opposites attract, smoking hot, mayhem and madness, romantic comedy. Oh, and one very naughty Maine Coon cat.

If you wish to learn of new releases from Elizabeth, sign up for her email newsletter.
Sign up at www.ElizabethSaFleur.com

ALSO BY ELIZABETH SAFLEUR

Sexy rom-coms:
The Sassy Nanny Dilemma
It Was All The Pie's Fault
It Was All the Cat's Fault
It Was All the Daisy's Fault

Short story collections:
Finally, Yours
Finally, His
Finally, Mine

Steamy Contemporary romance:
Tough Road
Tough Luck
Tough Break
Tough Love

Erotic romance with BDSM:
Elite
Holiday Ties
Untouchable
Perfect
Riptide
Lucky
Fearless
Invincible

Femme Domme:
The White House Gets A Spanking
Spanking the Senator

ABOUT THE AUTHOR

Elizabeth SaFleur writes award-winning, luscious romance from 28 wildlife-filled acres, hikes in her spare time and is a certifiable tea snob.

Find out more about Elizabeth on her web site at www.ElizabethSaFleur or join her private Facebook group, Elizabeth's Playroom.

Follow her on TikTok (@ElizabethSaFleurAuthor) and Instagram (@ElizabethLoveStory), too.